DEATH CALLED AT NIGHT

Jimmy Ellis believes his parents have died in a car crash when as a young boy he is taken to live with relatives in Australia. The years pass happily, then the nightmare comes. Terrifying images flit through his mind in the dark — all through the eyes of a child, a witness to grisly events seventeen years before. He begins to delve into the past, and soon he finds himself on the trail of a double murderer — a murderer who is prepared to kill again.

R. A. BENNETT

DEATH CALLED AT NIGHT

Complete and Unabridged

LINFORD
Leicester

First published in Great Britain in 1983 by
Robert Hale Limited
London

First Linford Edition
published 1999
by arrangement with
Robert Hale Limited
London

British Library CIP Data

Bennett, R. A. (Richard Alan), *1946*–
Death called at night.—Large print ed.—
Linford mystery library
1. Detective and mystery stories
2. Large type books
I. Title
823.9'14 [F]

ISBN 0–7089–5478–2

Published by
F. A. Thorpe (Publishing) Ltd.
Anstey, Leicestershire

Set by Words & Graphics Ltd.
Anstey, Leicestershire
Printed and bound in Great Britain by
T. J. International Ltd., Padstow, Cornwall

This book is printed on acid-free paper

1

The boy conjured new games in his head, anything to make the time pass more quickly; shifting restlessly, aware of the monotonous tick of the clock on the mantelpiece. The television bathed the corner of the room in silvery light, the sudden spurt of flame from the fire in the hearth threw wild and dancing shadows across the walls and ceiling.

The heat singed the boy's leg, felt good. He slipped further down the rug, allowed the fire to toast the length of his body. His eyes rolled sideways to the man and woman on the sofa. There was a distance between them tonight, a coldness. But then, this was nothing new. They argued often, and he was certain the man sometimes struck the woman. She cried a lot, never in his presence — but he knew.

He studied the shadows that crossed her face, noted the sadness in her eyes.

And the man? The boy sensed the man cared little for either of them. He wasn't interested in the coming football match. He constantly glanced at his watch. He would leave soon. He seldom stayed in. Perhaps this was the source of the arguments, or perhaps it was something deeper, something he wouldn't understand until he was older.

The music blared. The boy's eyes shot to the small screen; everything forgotten in this much anticipated moment. Soon. Oh, so soon. He knew his team would win. He wrapped his arms around his legs and drew his knees to his chin.

The rap on the back door was a shattering intrusion.

No one moved. Reluctantly, the boy shifted his eyes to the man and woman. They stared at each other icily, mute, challenging. Strangely, it was the man who shrugged, moved from the room.

The boy heard the click of a lock, felt the sudden draught that ran through the house. The fire spluttered. He shivered. He heard raised voices. He noted the frown on the woman's brow. She was standing now, moving towards the door.

The explosion seemed to shake the walls. The boy stiffened. The scene on the television screen was forgotten. The woman had gone from his view. He heard the beginnings of a scream that were strangled in a second explosion.

He sat rigid. He heard footsteps running down the side of the house. The sudden silence terrified him. Even the sound from the television had died.

It seemed hours before he was able to move. His limbs shook. He crept through the door, into the small kitchen. Grey light filtered through the open door, misty with rain, icy cold. He stumbled, straightened. He fell to his knees.

'Mum?'

His voice was shallow. The voice of a stranger. He shook her, raised her body. He brushed aside the hair that covered her face. Her eyes were open, darkest blue, penetrating deep inside himself.

'Mum?'

Her gold crucifix had caught in the corner of her mouth. He pulled it free. It glinted and flashed in the pale light.

He shook her again; softly, then violently. Still she didn't stir. His hands felt strange; warm and gluey. He looked down at them. The room filled with the wail of a soul in agony, beat across the walls, beat deep into his own mind until all reason fled.

2

I exploded from the black void.

I exploded into a world of brilliant light. I clamped my eyes shut to protect them from the glare, the golden blaze. My mouth opened, clogged with grit and sand, a thousand crusted sores. The noise still echoed around me. The noise of those demented ghouls that tormented me. Sweat scorched parched lips, sizzled on tender skin.

'Come on, love.'

The nails bit deep into my shoulders, claws of the eagle. I was carrion, soared through the hot desert air. The sting of a palm across my face took my breath away.

'I'm sorry.' The voice was frantic. 'But wake up, love.'

I took control. I breathed deeply. I was alive. No feast for the eagle. A nightmare. That was all. The same bloody nightmare that had haunted me for almost a year.

'You scared the living daylights out of me, love. I've never had that effect on a man before.'

My eyes came open, narrowed against the light, yet still the terror gripped my heart.

'Shall I make you a coffee, love?'

I nodded. Her talons freed themselves from my shoulders, hovered there, as if afraid I might topple over. She eased backwards, and stepped off the bed.

I listened to her movements in the kitchen. Heard the cupboard doors opening and closing as she searched. I breathed more steadily, rolled on my side, let my eyes wander to the window.

Sydney; pulse of the Lucky Country. Too bloody true. Blue sky, golden sun, shimmering rooftops; and out there, way in the distance, the deeper blue of the harbour water, the deeper gold of the sandy beaches. I loved this city.

The whispering crawl of contentment slipped away. The nightmare was with me again. The greyness, the black void. The faces were already beginning to blur, and I knew would soon disappear completely. The events would not. And the fear always lingered, the stark terror that stole through my mind in the night.

The boy in the nightmare had to be myself. How else could I have observed those terrible events through his eyes? But it was all wrong. My parents died in a car crash when I was eight years old. At least, that was what I always believed.

But wait!

My Aunt Edna and cousins never mentioned my parents. In fact, I never mentioned them. I asked no questions. It was as if they had never existed. I never thought of them because I had no memory of them. I had never cared what they were like, what they were. But I was beginning to care. The nightmare was making me care. I knew I had to discover the truth. I had to know my parents! I had to know how and why they died!

A mug was pushed into my hand. I allowed the liquid to trickle down my throat. It burned. I coughed. I wiped my mouth with the back of my hand. I rolled on my back and looked at her for the first time.

She hovered at the foot of the bed, lips moving as she searched for words that wouldn't come; naked, body neatly clipped into three sections by two startling slashes of white, highlighting the nipples and the dark triangular patch. Her hair was long and tousled and streaked by exposure to the sun, face open and friendly, skin firm against bone.

She studied me nervously. She tried to smile, turned a little, seeking approval. Words finally formed on her tongue.

'Yeah. Guess you're okay now, love.'

Who the hell was she?

Her face was that of a stranger. I tried to recall the previous evening. I remembered the pub, one of the mates mentioning a party. I remembered the house, the booze, the hostess with the big tits, the birds — then oblivion.

She seemed to have read my thoughts. The corner of her mouth turned down sulkily. She was suddenly coy, snatching her clothes from where she had tossed them on the floor.

'I'm sorry,' I managed to mumble.

The words croaked from my lips. And

infinite sympathy and compassion welled inside me, as much for myself as her. I needed her more than I had ever needed anyone before. Her back was to me as she tried to dress, all fingers and thumbs, desperate to be gone from this humiliation.

'For Christ's sake!' I yelled. 'I've just witnessed my parents being murdered!' Now I was the desperate one. I wanted her to understand. 'Do you know what it means to feel your mother's blood on your hands! Night after bloody night!'

Oh, sweet Jesus! What was I saying? But the words had the right effect.

She stilled, turned. She chewed her lip, considering. She came closer. I kissed her, pulled her tight, willing to use and give, but still wishing I could remember her name.

★ ★ ★

Lorries!

That was my first impression. Millions of the buggers. Thundering past, zipping remorselessly in the opposite direction.

And this was England, land of my birth. Green, cool, dark towns and cities, hazy drizzle, splashes of pale sunlight that disappeared even faster than they came. The motorway spun northwards, mile upon mile.

My mind drifted.

Maureen Donnelly, that was her name. I'd sneaked a look in her bag when she'd retired to the bathroom for repairs. Two hours after I'd erupted from my nightmare she'd walked from my flat, and my life. But I had had no time to dwell on Maureen.

I made some phone calls. Cousin Eric was on the bum in Queensland and I couldn't get through to him. I caught cousin Sal with the third call. And no, she didn't know how my parents had died, though she had a vague notion somebody had mentioned a car crash. She asked when I was coming over. I said I was on my way to England, and hung up. The decision was made.

There was a sharp and not so sweet interview with my boss. Leave? His smile was greasy. 'You know where you can stick your leave, don't you, old son?' I knew. Right up my — . But stuff that, and him.

I was through anyway. Journalist, announced my union card. Hell! Twenty-five and still no higher than an office boy. Maybe I wasn't good enough. Maybe I was the tosser the boss made me out to be. Maybe it was the nights on the booze. Who the hell knew? I didn't. Anyway, when I returned to Aussie I could always head north, bum around for a while, find cousin Eric, earn a crust here and there. I decided I should have chucked the job years ago.

I sold my car, my possessions, and collected my passport. I didn't know how long I'd be away. A week? A year? Now I didn't care.

The flight. Fine at first, then growing more tedious. Meals all the way, plastic and tasteless.

Heathrow, and the first murmurings of panic, a solitude, a stranger in a distant land, wondering what to do, where to go, lost. Two days in London. Unimpressed. A city without light. An ancient woman

11

too long on her own, too long with her memories; faceless crowds that never settled. But this wasn't my England. My roots lay in the north.

I hired a car, a fancy model to lighten my mood, and was soon on the motorway. Over two hundred miles and four hours later, I pulled off. An old and ancient city through which the Roman legions had once marched, less than ten miles from the town of my birth. I knew what I wanted and where to head.

I found the library section of the regional evening newspaper, and laid the newspapers out before me.

This was the England of the sixties. The Beatles ruled the pop world, Alf Ramsey ruled the England football team, London was swinging merrily, girls wore skirts that never quite managed to cover their behinds, hippies wore flowers in their hair and preached a peace they would never find.

I had a rough idea of the date, almost seventeen years ago. Late November. The deaths of two people in a traffic accident would merit a mention, if only a few brief words.

I found much more!

My blood chilled. A paralysis entered my body but failed to reach my trembling fingertips. The pain that shook me was almost tangible. No car crash. The nightmare had become reality.

The photographs were hazy, hard to discern the dim features. A man and woman, both in their twenties, a small boy between them. He stared straight into the camera. A small frown creased his brow. A familiar pose I had seen many times before, staring back at me from the mirror.

I was that boy!

I quickly wiped away a tear that stung my eye. I breathed deeply, concentrated on the print.

My parents were slain in the kitchen of their home. They died from severe shotgun wounds. The boy was in the house, but not thought to have seen the killer. He had suffered a lapse of memory.

There was some vague speculation on

13

the motive for the murders. Nothing concrete. In one story, written a fortnight after the deaths, it stated that the police had made no arrests, and the investigation was proceeding slowly; which in their cryptic jargon meant they were completely baffled. From there on the amount of space given to the story began to taper off.

There was a brief mention that the boy was being cared for by his grandmother. That brought bile to my throat. I remembered that old woman all right. I remembered my fear of her, the taste of her nearness. I remembered the blessed day when Aunt Edna snatched me away.

I pushed the newspapers aside, made a note of the journalist's name, and wearily made my way upstairs.

A familiar scene. A newsroom much the same as the one in which I had worked in Sydney; smaller, more antique, but basically the same; a picture of activity and sloth. I asked for Larry Jenkins and a finger pointed me in the right direction. He listened half-heartedly for a few seconds, then it dawned on him who I was and he sat up. I had his attention.

We retired to the pub next door, lunched on cold pie and warm beer. He was a man of some fifty years, running to fat, smelling of a life that had turned sour, but his tired eyes were friendly and comradely.

I recounted the nightmare, the purpose of my visit to England. There was a gap in my life I needed to fill. He listened without interruption. He had no words of comfort.

'Still no memory?' he asked. 'Only the nightmare?'

'That's right. And the sequence of events in the nightmare fit the facts, don't they?'

'Almost exactly.' He studied me. 'This stuff you've been giving me. This search for your roots. Are you sure you're not here on some holy crusade, chum?'

'Hardly.' I smiled weakly. 'Until an hour ago, I didn't even know how my parents died. The nightmare scared the shit out of me. It had me almost convinced. But I didn't know until I read those newspapers. More than anything I came to England to plug those missing eight years.' Abruptly, my mind changed tack. There was a sudden rage inside me. 'But why shouldn't I embark on this holy crusade you mentioned. Some bastard butchered them. And if he's not gone to his grave with the secret, he's still walking around. And perhaps if he isn't put behind bars the nightmare will haunt me the rest of my life. That really does scare me, old sport. Ever been literally dead on your feet yet too scared to lay your head on the pillow? I have to be pissed before I can even face a bed!'

Perturbed by my outburst, he shifted uneasily. We talked around in circles for a while, then he got to the point.

'The murders occurred in Penningstone,' he said. 'A small town of some fourteen thousand inhabitants ten miles east of here. The police turned it upside down, then moved on to Saddlebridge. That is the village where your father was born, and where he spent a lot of his time.'

I remembered Saddlebridge. I lived

there for some months with my grand-mother and uncle. It was not a memory I relished.

'Old Charlie Grey led the initial investigation,' he went on. 'He concentrated on Saddlebridge.' I asked why, and he shrugged. 'I couldn't say. Charlie probably had a bee in his bonnet. The police turned up more firearms than the Texans had at the Alamo, licensed and otherwise, but if they ever had their hands on the murder weapon they couldn't prove it.

'It was a major crime, and brought huge press and TV coverage. Too big for the local police, and in less than a week old Charlie was shunted out. A Chief Super and a new team arrived. They had different ideas. They ignored Saddlebridge.

'And nobody will ever know what was going on in Charlie's mind. He died when his car spun off the road, only a couple of months after the murders.

'I followed him to Saddlebridge in those early days.' His face soured in disgust. 'Hardly half an hour's drive

17

from here yet it might have been another planet. Outsiders were not welcome. And they surely didn't welcome the press. I stayed at a place called the Fox Inn. A weird set-up. Owned by a youngish chap named George Slater. There was an invalid woman who never left her bed, and spent most of her time thumping on the ceiling with her stick. There was the woman's daughter — Sarah. She was really something. She could pop the buttons off your pants from twenty yards range. I couldn't believe it when they told me she was no more than fourteen.

'And it's funny you should turn up in the flesh.' My eyebrows rose in question. 'Oh, nothing dramatic; just that about a year ago the editor decided to resurrect the story. He used one of the women. She returned with little more than a rehash of what had gone before. Anyway, to explain my earlier remark — she wanted to interview you. The cheeky bitch wanted us to send her to Australia.'

'Does she still work here?'

He shook his head. 'She moved to London. Television. One day I expect

I'll see her reading the news. And she'll have earned her promotion between the sheets.'

He didn't try to disguise the bitterness in his voice. He turned a little shifty when I asked what he knew about my parents. On the subject of my mother he had little to say. About my father, more. My father had the reputation of being something of a rogue, and certainly one of the local rams.

There was little more information he could impart, though he gave me the name of an old mate of his at the local nick in Penningstone.

★ ★ ★

Not an impressive town, Penningstone. Stone and brick terraces straddling either side of the valley, bisected by a narrow river. Old buildings, a small shopping centre, no office blocks.

The police station stood on the main road; a bleak facade that resembled a Victorian workhouse. Inside, the electric heaters did little to relieve the chill.

I found myself seated opposite a man of around forty. He was Detective Sergeant Patrick Cooper. I mentioned Larry Jenkins and he laid aside the folder he had been studying. I repeated the story I had given Jenkins. He leaned back in a casual pose, fingers entwined behind his neck.

'It takes me back,' he said. 'I'd just gone into plain clothes. I remember you. I was there when old Charlie first spoke to you at the hospital. You resembled a little corpse. You didn't remember a thing, as if someone had wiped your mind clear. Old Charlie tried twice more, then gave up.'

We went into more details, then I asked if it was true that Charlie Grey concentrated on Saddlebridge.

'That's right.' He nodded. 'You went to live there with your grannie at the local post office and store. Not that you were seen much. Your uncle took you to and from school, and you never left the building otherwise.'

I remembered, and my blood chilled a little. I was almost a prisoner in that

20

house. I asked why Charlie Grey had been so interested in Saddlebridge.

'Blowed if I know.' He shrugged. 'We were following Charlie's nose. He was a loner who wouldn't have survived in the force today, but there was room for a character like Charlie then. So if he decided the killer lived in Saddlebridge, that was good enough. He was a starving dog with a meaty bone. He interviewed every last person.

'Then Charlie got the bullet. His methods were too slow and tedious. The glory boys moved in. Still, Charlie didn't quit. There were complaints from the villagers. Charlie was on the carpet several times. He didn't give a tinker's cuss. So although he was off the enquiry officially, he wasn't deterred. He even hinted that he knew the identity of the killer.' He smiled. 'There is a legend around here that Charlie's ghost still haunts Saddlebridge.

'The glory boys were soon stumped; ideas as scarce as rocking-horse shit. Their only chance was that the killer might strike again. But he had already done his dirty business.'

I asked for more details of Charlie Grey's death. He smiled and shook his head.

'Nothing like that, mate. Charlie liked to booze, and he was never the best driver in the world. He had a gutful of whisky inside him when he spun his car off the road.'

There were more facts; but facts I wasn't too keen on hearing.

'A bit of a rascal was Pete,' he informed me, not having to make it plain that Pete was my father. 'In his teens he ran around with a gang that specialised in wrecking pubs and cafes. He had a spell on probation after he and a mate broke into a shop and nicked a few thousand fags. He married, seemed to have settled down. Then there was a series of break-ins. We rounded up the most likely lads — Pete included; the jobs had his clumsy hallmark written all over them. We couldn't make anything stick, so he walked away. Coincidence or otherwise, the break-ins ceased with his death.'

I asked if the break-ins could have been connected with the murders.

'A falling out of thieves?' He shrugged. 'No. A two-man effort. Corner shops owned by old ladies. They couldn't have netted more than a hundred quid all totted up. And if Pete was involved, his accomplice had to be Dave Pearson, an old cronie from way back. We grilled Dave, but got nothing from him.' He paused. 'Whatever you want to know about Pete, Dave is your boy, and an honest man these days. You'll find him on the building site around the corner.'

There was still more.

'The killings might not have been a spur of the moment crime. It was Wednesday. In those days this town boasted a cinema. It was almost a ritual that your mum took you there Wednesday evenings. But this particular Wednesday there was an important football game on television. And you were football mad. It seems pretty certain that you and your mum were in the house that night because the football was being broadcast live. The killer probably thought Pete was alone.

Your mum was unlucky. She shouldn't have been there.'

That made me a little sick, and more than sad. He gave me directions to the house in Livingstone Terrace where the murders had taken place, and the name of the woman who lived next door. If I needed help I could phone him. I told him I'd probably go to Saddlebridge and snoop around for a while, get the feel of the land. I thanked him, and left.

3

'Why don't you piss off back to where you came from, mate!'

I couldn't begin to figure out his aggressive attitude. I only knew the effect it had on me. Dave Pearson, once my father's best friend, turned his back and began to toss the jagged bricks into a wheelbarrow. I gripped his shoulder and spun him around. My fists bunched at my sides. His watery eyes took me in and he shrugged.

'I'm not going to fight you, mate,' he said quietly. 'I knew you when you were a nipper. Your old man was my mate. So swing away, and I hope it gives you some comfort.'

That deflated me. I stepped back, feeling foolish, began to relax. I tried again.

'About the time my dad died there were a number of break-ins in this area. Two men involved. My dad was one; a little bird informs me that you were the other.'

'And this little bird plods a beat and blows a little tin whistle,' he said drily. 'And I've been through this many times. Old Charlie Grey himself even tried. I gave him no answers, nor will I give them to you. There have been others sniffing along the same trail. Reporters. The last only a year back. Little more than a chit of a girl. I advised her into which particular orifice she should stick her five pounds bounty money.'

'Does it matter now,' I said reasonably. 'Seventeen years — the police will hardly be interested — .'

'The bogies are always interested. And hasn't it got through your thick head yet — the old life is behind me. I have a wife and kid of my own now. I don't care about the past. Pete is dead and buried. I don't want to talk about him, not even to you. I don't know who killed him, or why, and now I don't give a damn. Let sleeping dogs lie, mate.'

I pressed on. I wanted details of my father's life, anything. He refused to budge. Then he surprised me.

'Okay,' he said wearily. 'This is something I've never mentioned before. Vic Hanson. He worked at the brewery the same time as Pete. And Pete mentioned that he and Hanson were working a fiddle. But don't ask me what fiddle because I don't know. It was something Pete let slip when he'd had too much to drink. I didn't give it much thought at the time. But about a year after Pete died I heard that Hanson had been given the boot from the brewery for thieving. That is all I know.'

'You told the police?'

'Don't make me laugh. And like I said, I didn't give it much thought.' I asked what he knew of Hanson, but his lips had stiffened again. 'Not a lot. Only that he lives in Saddlebridge.'

Again, I tried to get him to open up about my parents. But again he refused. The past was buried, he continued to repeat. I gave up. But I had the gut feeling I'd be talking to Dave Pearson again before very long.

★ ★ ★

I didn't use the car. I walked.

Livingstone Terrace was a narrow street on the edge of town, winding up the hill with perhaps a dozen neat stone cottages on either side, the doors painted in muted colours, lace curtains at the small windows.

I paused outside number fifteen. No fresh paint here. The windows were thick with dust. I turned, viewed the street from this angle.

I must have stood here a thousand times or more. I'd be eight years old then, and I tried to transpose my mind backwards into that of a child. No memories flooded back, no pain, no delights.

I moved on and knocked on number seventeen. The door opened tentatively. She was small and elderly, and smelling how little old ladies were supposed to smell — crisp and clean.

'Mrs Atkinson?' I asked.

She nodded, curious. I told her the police had given me her name. Her eyes registered fright. I smiled.

'It's okay,' I assured her. 'I'm Jimmy Ellis.'

A blankness covered her face. The name meant nothing to her. She waited for me to explain. I repeated my name. I once lived next door, number fifteen.

'Little Jimmy!' she exclaimed.

I was soon inside with a glass of sherry in my hand. She talked, and talked. Did I remember such and such an event? Did I remember this and that? It meant nothing to me. I had no memory of this street, or her. But I nodded, and listened, and smiled to fill in the appropriate pauses.

Eventually, I told her the truth. I had no recollection of my life in this street. She patted my hand and apologised for her thoughtlessness. I assured her I had enjoyed listening to her reminiscences. I asked for more details about my parents. She sat quietly for a while as she considered.

'I liked your mother — Jenny,' she said finally. 'You will already have gathered that. A bit reserved, but very friendly and kind.' She met my eyes. 'I never saw much of Pete. The odd good morning, no more. He worked for the brewery, drove a delivery lorry. He drank quite a bit. I often heard him shouting and swearing. There is little more I can add.'

I wasn't sure how to put this question. 'They tell me he was something of a womaniser?'

'There was gossip.' Her eyes remained steady. 'And certainly he was a handsome man with that special spark of mischief in his eye. And as I look at you closer, it might almost be as if I was seeing him again. The resemblance is uncanny.'

I shifted uncomfortably. I asked about the night my parents died.

'I heard raised voices, then the shots,' she said, voice lowering. 'A car back-firing I thought at first. Then the footsteps ran down the back of the house. I was puzzled, so I opened the back door but could see nothing. Then I heard this terrible scream. I ran to your house. The kitchen door was open but there was no light on. Something blocked the doorway but I had no time for that. My eyes were fixed on you. You were kneeling on the floor. You were screaming as if a million demons were at war within you.'

She paused. The room went silent. We both wanted that silence, yet both knew she had to go on.

'Jenny's head rested in your lap. You were holding up your hands. They were dark with blood. The next I knew I was shaking you. That's when Mr Jones from the other side arrived. There was a burst of light as he flicked down the switch. He was mumbling under his breath. 'Oh, my God.' Over and over he said it. He guided us outside. I brought you here. Soon the street was alive with policemen and ambulances. The doctor gave you a sedative and they took you to the hospital.'

She took a deep breath, fixed her eyes in her lap. My guts twisted with rage and despair.

My first conscious memory was waking in that hospital. The whiteness, the pale faces of the doctors and nurses. Only the policeman disturbed me. A man who I could now put a name to. Charlie Grey. He asked questions. I closed my eyes

31

and refused to think, to remember. I kept wishing he'd go away, and finally he did.

Then there was grandmother. She said things about my mother, bad things. Yet somehow it didn't hurt. I had turned a key in my brain. I had no mother. My mother never existed, had no face, no voice, so how could I be hurt? But I hated my grandmother. I hated her home that was my prison. I hated everything about my life then except for Uncle Frank. Then my Aunt Edna had taken me to the other side of the world.

There was little more to say to Mrs Parkinson. Again I paused outside number fifteen, took in the dusty windows, the flaked paint. I wondered if anybody had lived there since the tragedy, if the house had remained unoccupied for seventeen years. It seemed strange. So long ago now. I wondered who owned the house. I could feel Mrs Atkinson's curious eyes in the middle of my back, and for a second almost turned to ask her about the house. I didn't. I wanted to get away from here, quickly.

★ ★ ★

The fresh breeze and morning air did something to revive my spirits, if only marginally.

Yesterday had been tiring, and putting it mildly, traumatic. After leaving Livingstone Terrace, I had walked, then walked some more. The night stole up on me. The street lights sparked into life. The pavements emptied of people. I spotted the notice in the window. ROOMS TO LET.

Hardly more than a flea-pit for the desperate, but I booked in. I was shown to a pokey and grim room. I lay on the bed, lost in my thoughts. The curtains were open. I watched the sky turn black, heard the sudden lash of a storm. I drifted into a shallow sleep.

The nightmare returned.

I awoke screaming, bathed in sweat, desperate to shake the blood from my hands. A fist hammered on the wall. A less than compassionate voice called for me to pipe down or he'd fill my mouth with his boot. There was no nameless girl to comfort me now. I was alone, totally and absolutely alone. I didn't try to sleep again.

Now, I leaned back against the car, allowing the breeze to cleanse away the last of the nightmare.

The brewery where my father had worked stood before me, sooty brick and mortar, and the largest employer in Penningstone since the last of the cotton mills had closed.

It didn't take me long to find the personnel office.

The girl was in her twenties, and could only be described as attractively plain. None of her features seemed quite right, too big or too small, or the wrong shape, but tossed together and mixed indiscriminately they added up to something that was definitely unique. At the moment she was a little harassed. The telephone rang constantly, a male voice continually bellowed from behind a closed door. So she had little time to spare for me.

I told her I was seeking information on two ex-employees, a James Peter Ellis, and a Vic Hanson, the man Dave Pearson had mentioned; especially I wanted to know why Hanson left the company's employment. I embellished my requests with a few well-chosen untruths. She shook her head.

'Impossible,' she repeated for the fourth time. 'We don't give out such information.' I asked why. She shrugged, confused. 'It just isn't done.' She nodded to the closed door from where the voice came. 'You should really be asking him, but I wouldn't advise it.'

'You do keep your ex-employees' records?'

'In the basement. They go back seventy years.'

'You will look for me?' I used my best smile, and she thawed a little. 'I'd be grateful.'

'I dare say.' Her eyes held a glint of interest. 'But you still haven't explained why you want to look at them.'

I had. But every time I tried the phone rang, or the man bellowed. I explained that one of the men was my father, the other a friend of his. I wanted to check the dates and suchlike. I was a writer and just back from Australia. I was writing a history of my family. She was pondering, then the phone rang again. She was saying she'd be there immediately. She stood, shrugged to me.

'You'll have to go,' she said. 'Come back next week.'

Next week was a long way off, but I had time to spare.

* * *

I crossed the Pennines into Yorkshire. The hills became moors, then dissolved into a series of faceless towns and cities that seemed to have no beginning and no end; smoke and tall chimneys, shiny glass office blocks and car-parks. It was a long and tedious drive that took me to my destination.

Joy? Delight?

Aunt Edna pulled me tight. Kisses poured down, mixed with tears. Questions. What was I doing in England? Why hadn't I written? How were Eric and Sal? I answered only in short bursts when she paused for breath.

The happiest moments of my life were wrapped up in this woman; my beloved Aunt Edna. She had been everything to me, mother, sister, friend. She had changed little in the six years since I had last seen her. A little more silver in the hair, a little plumper, perhaps only now losing her dogged campaign against a spreading waistline.

It was she who had taken me to Australia, and made me part of her family. Her, Uncle Alex, my cousins Eric and Sal. Eleven happy years. Then came the death of Uncle Alex and the disintegration of the family. Aunt Edna returned to the England she secretly always yearned for. She could do no more for her family. Eric, Sal, and I stayed on in Australia.

We talked endlessly. Evening came. Now I sensed the pain would begin. I could have come to her as soon as I arrived in England, but I needed to be alone when I learned the truth of my parents' deaths; when the events of the nightmare would be confirmed to me, as deep down I knew they would be. And I wanted to relieve her of the burden of telling me herself. I wanted to cause this woman no grief.

I recounted the nightmare; how I had spent the last two days. I studied her in the fading light of evening. Her skin had paled. Her small hands had become fists and I knew scarlet nails punctured white skin. She stood, moved about the room. Her movements were as wooden as those of a manipulated puppet.

'Go home, Jimmy. Go back to Australia.'

I hardly recognised her voice. I couldn't believe those icy tones belonged to Aunt Edna.

'Why did you say they died in a car crash, Edna?' I asked. 'Why did you lie?'

'I never lied to you!' She spun to face me. 'I never said they died that way. You did! On the plane that took us from England. You called me auntie. A woman in front heard and asked if you were being taken to your mother and father. You told her they had died in a car smash. That was the first and only time I heard it spoken. You showed

38

no curiosity about them, Jimmy. Not one tiny iota. I decided that was a blessing. Their deaths were too horrible to contemplate. And you were there when they died. You witnessed the brutality of their end. Go home, Jimmy. Forget them.'

'Will the nightmare let me forget, Edna?' A fury rose inside me. 'This very morning I awoke in the dark with her blood on my hands. The terror I experience is real. I want the bastard who did it! I now know that is the only way I can destroy the nightmare. I am a haunted man. Don't you understand that, Edna!'

'Seventeen years!' She faced me. Her fury matched mine. 'The police couldn't find him! So what chance have you? I see the light of a fanatic in your eyes and it scares me. You are embarking on something that I believe will destroy you. Pure hate is motivating you, Jimmy!'

'You still haven't answered, Edna. The nightmare. I've lived with it for almost a year. How do I rid myself of that?'

'I don't know. But you being here,

raking up the past, won't help. And there are doctors. They — .'

'Oh, Christ! A head shrinker I suppose!' I yelled. 'Now you think I'm a bloody lunatic!'

'I don't.' She was sobbing, hugging me now. She pressed my head to her breast. 'But this isn't the way. It will consume you. Don't you see that?'

The battle was over. We sat quietly. I asked her about my parents, for an insight into their personalities. She shook her head sadly.

'I will not help you destroy yourself,' she said firmly. 'Under other circumstances I would be happy to talk to you about them. At one time, I even wanted you to ask, but not now, not while you are hell-bent on revenge, not while you have this hate in your heart.'

I tried to get her to change her mind. She remained adamant. She was as stubborn as Dave Pearson had been the day before. I stayed the night. I met her new husband. I liked him, and he obviously loved Edna, and I thanked God for that.

4

I didn't pause in Penningstone. I drove straight through, took the road that led into the dark hills and the next valley. I was a man in search of his beginnings; a man in search of a double killer. So why not follow in the footsteps of Charlie Grey? It was a starting point.

Less than three miles as the crow flies and I gazed down on Saddlebridge.

There were something like seventy buildings, straggling along two narrow roads that met in the centre of the village, sloping upwards in the distance. There were few landmarks: the tiny church, the village cross, the small stone bridge. The hills loomed all around, colours switching from green to purple to brown at the blink of an unsuspecting eyelid. I shivered.

I remembered Saddlebridge. In a sense my life had begun here, aged eight. I remembered the stormy skies and hills, the cold wind that whipped along the streets.

I drove over the stone bridge and pulled onto the car-park at the side of a tall stone building on the edge of the village. I glanced up at the sign that swung in the breeze. The Fox Inn. The year underneath read 1851.

I collected my bags from the boot and moved to the front door. Inside, two more doors confronted me. The door on my right had SALOON BAR stencilled on the glass. I opened the door on my left. I allowed my eyes to adjust to the dimness. A long passage stretched before me, empty, cool, smelling of old wood and varnish. There were doors on either side, solid and low, the floor creaked under my feet with every step. I wondered if the place was deserted, decided it couldn't possibly be so.

'Can I help you?'

I almost jumped through my skin, spun around. A man in his forties; tall, deep lines etched into his face, eyes almost invisible under bushy brows; the face of a mad undertaker. His voice was deep and powerful.

'You looking for something?'

Was this George Slater? The reporter Larry Jenkins said he was a youngish bloke, but that was seventeen years ago, which would make his present age about right. The man gave me the shivers. I shrugged, tried to smile.

'I hope so, sport. I'd like a room.'

'Not much entertainment around here for a young fellow,' he pointed out unhelpfully.

'Peace and quiet, sport. That's just what I need.'

He scowled, eyes flicking over me, obviously unimpressed. He turned, ducked and passed through a doorway. I presumed it was my cue to follow. A small office at the side of the building. The window overlooked the car-park. The man must have seen me arrive. So why had he allowed me to linger in the passage? I decided it was probably no more than a surliness of character. I signed the register with a flourish.

'George?'

The voice came from the passage. The door opened.

'Oh, we have — .' Her mouth fell

open. The tray she carried in the crook of her arm crashed to the floor. I found her reaction to my face fascinating.

I asked, 'I'm not that ugly, am I, love?'

She shook her head. 'You remind me of someone, sweetheart, that's all.'

Her voice was light and pleasant, teasing. The scowl on the man's face deepened. His voice was a growl as he offered to show me upstairs. Back into the passage, a narrow and dark staircase with a turn close to the top. He pushed open a door. Then he was gone.

It was a large room. A bed, wardrobe, dresser, a small table and chair under the window. I was at the back of the building. Underneath, a paved yard stretched into an expansive but uncultivated garden. Blankets on the clothes-line flapped in the wind. The clouds had begun to close in and now I could barely make out the summits of the hills in the evening mist, though the patchwork of lanes and small stone walls were clearly defined. Memories began to stir, slip away. A strange tranquillity swept over me. I felt as though I had stepped through a door into another world.

I lay on the bed, let time drift. An hour passed. There was the patter of feet on the stairs, the rap of knuckles. The door opened without invitation and she stepped inside. She smiled, leaned her back to the door. I put her age at thirty. Fetchingly untidy brown hair flowed over her shoulders, breasts full and high, hips wide and provocatively thrusting. She wasn't beautiful, but certainly sensual, and definitely sexual. My examination brought a flash of amusement to her eyes. Again, I recalled Larry Jenkins, and his description of a fourteen year old girl.

'I guess you must be Sarah,' I said. Her head cocked to one side in question. 'Oh, someone I met. He mentioned this place. The landlord, a young girl and her invalid mother.'

'It sounds as if this someone is a little out of date.' The amused sparkle never left her eyes. 'My mother died thirteen years ago. George is my husband now.'

I found that a little sad, and disappointing. I asked why George hadn't been keen on having me stay here. She came deeper into the room. I caught the smell of her. A touch of perfume, and more — raw sex. It was a heady aroma.

'George is never keen on letting rooms. He sees it as an invasion of our privacy, strangers living on the same floor as ourselves. And he gets lazy. Only the two of us and a barmaid who turns up when the mood takes her. In Summer, there is just too much to do. The car trade, the hikers, the bikers. Thankfully, we are drifting towards Winter. We can be cut off for days when the snows come. Only the regulars then.'

I asked who she thought I was when she first saw me.

'I think you know.' She was very close now. I could have reached out and touched her. 'He would have been about the age you are now when he died, wouldn't he? It was as if he had suddenly come back to life.'

We were obviously talking about my

father. I asked how well she had known him.

'Not well.' She tossed her head and her hair billowed. A strange sight in the stillness of this room. 'I'd be in my early teens. He came to the village to visit his mother, then here for a drink. Two or three times a week. You lived here for a while, didn't you? After they died? I don't remember ever seeing you.'

I pointed out that I rarely left grandmother's house. She nodded thoughtfully. She asked why I had come back. I had already concocted my lie.

'I work on a newspaper in Sydney. I received a telephone call about a year ago. A reporter. She was trying to get a new angle on the murders. I wasn't interested. I still have no memory of my early life. I told her so. Anyway, some time later I mentioned it to my editor. He decided to send me back. Saddlebridge seemed a good starting point.'

'It must be costing a great deal of money?'

'Worth it though. Think, the son of

47

the victims solving the mystery seventeen years later. There will be big money in that.' I watched her toss her hair from her shoulders and fold her arms. 'Did the reporter stay here?'

'No, but she came to the pub a couple of times.' She smiled softly. 'She pushed herself at the men but it got her nowhere. She soon returned to where she came from.'

I wondered if there was a hint in her words — for me — if I would soon be returning to where I came from? She glanced at her watch. If I wished to be fed I was to come down in half an hour. George would be opening the pub soon. She paused by the door, rattled the handle. No key. Never been necessary. She smiled. If I was frightened I should push a chair under the door handle. There was a small safe in the office and if I had any valuables she would lock them away. She left the room, but the scent of her lingered on.

* * *

The morning was glorious. The cool wind that ruffled my hair felt good. The late Autumn sun was bright in my face. The hills were sharp and clear against a blue sky, flickering into shadow as the sparse white clouds crossed the path of the sun.

I had spent a moderately comfortable evening and dreamless night. A good meal, a few drinks.

And I'm a nosy sort of bloke. I got my bearings. There were three bars. The saloon bar, the lounge bar, and a small bar at the back the locals referred to as the taproom. The saloon and lounge bars had been modernised in recent times. Both these bars were connected. The taproom could only be entered from the passage, and was screened off from the other bars. The living quarters were on the side of the building nearest the car-park. They were marked PRIVATE.

I spent the early evening in the saloon bar. It wasn't too crowded, but very noisy. Young people mostly. The turns-up-when-the-mood-takes-her barmaid was a talkative young piece named Lesley.

Every so often George or Sarah put in an appearance to make sure nobody was tearing the place apart. I was in no mood for frivolity.

I retired to the taproom at the back of the pub, which I guessed had hardly changed in a hundred years. The furniture was old and worn, a coal fire roared in the grate. The patrons were older here, and locals to a man. I sat in a corner and studied them. They drank, smoked, shared a joke, and yet not a single one of them glanced my way. It was as though I didn't exist. I found this curious. Perhaps my approach was wrong. Perhaps I should have thrust myself forward. But I sensed this would have been even more disastrous. So I sat on in my lonely corner. Only Sarah approached me, and only then to replenish my empty glass.

Now, the morning after, I took deep lungfuls of fresh air, strolled slowly to the heart of the village. My eyes took in the stone cottages, the small windows, the lace curtains. Not many people about. A few women who didn't even glance my way, the occasional passing car. Again, it seemed as though I was invisible; an alien caught in a strange time warp. It was eerie. Everything around me was normal, or would have been — but for me — the intruder.

My hand twisted the knob, a bell tinkled above my head and I was inside. A million strands of dust leapt and danced in the shafts of golden light that flooded through the window.

An old fear squeezed my heart. I wanted to turn and run. I didn't. I was a grown man now. I swallowed, closed my eyes and opened them.

I was eight years old again, stepping through that same door for the first time, chest thick with anguish, unable to comprehend what was happening to me. Then there were the clawed fingers that gripped my wrist. Then the force of the palm that rocked my head. If I didn't cease yelping I would get another. I ceased yelping.

I continued to stare around me. The rows of bottles that held the different coloured sweets might have been the same that stood on the same shelves those seventeen long years ago. In the corner was the wooden counter and grille that served as the post office.

Still no one had appeared. I began to sweat lightly. I moved back to the door, deciding to return later, postpone the meeting I knew would test my nerve and resolve. Again, the bell tinkled above my head. But too late to escape. The swish of a curtain, the tones of an old voice.

'Yes?'

I turned slowly. I tried to smile but my lips froze. I recognised her immediately, but she wasn't as she should have been. Her face was less sharp, even gentle; her hair short and soft and not long and frizzled. And she wasn't as old as I remembered, which struck me as odd. Seventy at most, which meant she was in her early fifties when I lived here. She had seemed at least a hundred years old to me then.

'Yes?' she repeated.

The voice had risen impatiently, though less shrill than I remembered, almost normal. Her eyes had narrowed, and I realised I was standing by the window with the sun behind me. I took a deep breath.

'Hello, grandmother.' I was startled by the normality of my voice.

'What did you call me?' she asked softly.

I came closer. Only the counter separated us.

'Who are you?' Her voice had risen again. I knew she was seeing me plainly. I read many emotions on her face, but none I could clearly discern. She repeated, 'Who are you?'

Doubts seized me, anger that I was being denied. 'Jimmy, grandmother. I carry the same name as your son. James Peter Ellis. He used the Peter. I use the James.'

'You cannot be him. You speak oddly.'

'Australian, grandmother. You recall Edna, my mother's sister? She took me away from here, away from you.'

'I recall,' she admitted. I was real to her now.

'No hugs and kisses, grandmother,' I said drily.

'So you haven't changed,' she said softly, almost sadly. 'Still surly and resentful. No pity in your heart for me.'

I was stunned. Everything had gone haywire. The seventeen year old memories were ashes in my mind. I asked what she meant.

'You left me. I who cared for you.'

'I was eight years old,' I mumbled, astonished, then angry. 'But I was glad Edna took me, grandmother. I hated this place! I hated you!'

She flinched, looked ancient. But there was wild sincerity in her eyes, the strength of a zealot. 'I did my best for you. I had to make you understand.'

'Understand what, grandmother?' No response, then I saw something. And I swear to God it was a tear. 'Tell me, grandmother! Tell me why you slapped my face!'

'Once! In anger and pain! That first day! I had lost a son. And you had to learn respect. You had to learn to love me properly.'

Love her! The idea revolted me. She

had hated me as a child. It was something I understood, something to cling on to. But had I been wrong? No, that couldn't be. She couldn't possibly have loved me. I could still hear and feel the bitterness of her words spoken so long ago.

'Your mother was a whore. She trapped your father — with you. But you won't be like her. I'll beat the bad blood from you.'

And now, as I stared at her, my mind whirled.

'Your room is still here,' she was saying.

Nothing was as I expected. I told her I had a room at the Fox Inn. A cloud crossed her face. Anger? Disappointment? It could have been either or both. Then the bell tinkled and a woman entered. Grandmother snatched up the counter flap and gestured me through.

I pulled aside the curtain and pushed open the door. The room hadn't changed. The same furniture, the same ornaments on the mantelpiece, the same darkened range. I went through the back into the large vegetable garden. The sun glinted on the greenhouse at the bottom.

He dropped the spade as soon as he saw me. He was tall and ungainly, his face as round as one of his prize turnips, cheeks ruddy from the wind and rain.

'Jimmy.' His face split in a wide grin. 'I heard you were back, wondered when you'd call.'

Uncle Frank, elder brother of my father. He made a living on this plot of land, helped grandmother in the store. He survived, ran his ancient Land Rover, and that was all he seemed to ask from life. He took me in a friendly bear hug before he released me.

We talked. I told him about Australia, my life. He never interrupted, never asked a single question as we sat on the log behind the greenhouse, our backs to the stone wall that surrounded the plot. I recalled the old days. The racks of sweets that were all around that were always denied me. Sweets were bad for my teeth. Sweets made pimples. But Uncle Frank sneaked me sweets, even if they were a little grubby after being in his pockets. I asked how he had known I was back.

Apparently it was the talk of the village. And the reason I was here was also known. I was now a journalist, and here to dig up the past. And if Uncle Frank knew this, so did grandmother. I pondered on the strange pantomime she had enacted back there and mentioned it to Uncle Frank.

'She probably lost her bearings,' he said. 'She'd have known who you were all right. She was excited last night. She cleaned out your old room for you.'

It seemed I had spent the last hour beating myself over the head with a cricket bat. Nothing made sense. It wasn't the grandmother I remembered. That grandmother should have been spitting in my eye, and that was the reception I'd expected when I walked into the post office. I asked Frank why she had treated me so badly when I was a kid.

His explanation was jumbled and inadequate. He added that it would take someone a lot brighter than himself to explain. And I guessed that was true. I asked him about my parents.

'Oh.' He poked the dark earth he loved with a stick. 'I seldom saw your mother. She never came here. Just the odd occasion in Penningstone.'

'And my father?'

'Hard to say.' A strange expression crossed his face. For a moment I could have sworn I saw hatred there. 'He was my brother, but we didn't get on. Personal reasons, Jimmy. Not really any concern of yours.'

Another brick wall. I returned to my mother. 'I've met no one who has a bad word to say about her, yet grandmother used to call her a whore. I remember that. I didn't even know what it meant at the time.'

He shrugged. He had no answer.

My mind slipped off at a tangent. I recounted my reception in the taproom last night. Uncle Frank didn't think it strange. I was born close by, but still a stranger. It would take time to earn their friendship.

Their friendship I could do without. We lunched in the kitchen. With grandmother present there was little conversation. We ate in a strained silence that jarred the nerves.

5

City life and the automobile had made me soft. I had walked less than three miles yet my limbs ached as if I had run a marathon. My scenic ramble complete, I limped back to the Fox Inn. There were few customers in the saloon bar. Lesley was on duty. I didn't linger. A quick drink to quench my thirst, then up to my room to rest my weary legs.

I attempted to read a book, but found it impossible. I was too restless. I went downstairs.

Lesley was in the passage, donning her coat. She seemed quite content to tarry. I asked if she knew a Vic Hanson. She certainly did. Vic lived not fifty yards from this very spot, and happened to be her best friend's uncle. Not that she liked him. Too free and fresh with his hands. I smiled along with her, encouraged her to talk.

'No home to go to, Lesley?'

Sarah had appeared from the office. There was a stiffness in her voice that Lesley recognised. The girl tossed her head haughtily and snapped her goodbyes. Sarah eyed me for a few seconds, then smiled.

'Lesley is a tease,' she said quietly. 'Only a wedding ring will buy you what you want from her.'

She slipped back into the office and closed the door without another word. I decided Sarah was a mystery I would dearly love to unravel.

★ ★ ★

'I did not get the sack! I found myself a better job!'

Vic Hanson kept me on the doorstep. A small man, well into his fifties, he seemed to strain on his toes to produce every last centimetre of height. I recognised him as one of the men in the taproom last night.

'Sweeping floors in a mill is better than poncing around in a security officer's uniform at the brewery?' I laughed drily.

'You must take me for an idiot, Vic.'

'You are an idiot!' he hissed.

I knew quite a bit about Vic Hanson, thanks to Lesley. I knew he had moved on from the brewery to Penningstone mill to toil as a labourer. I knew he was declared redundant when the mill closed and he hadn't worked since.

'Tell me about the fiddle you worked with my dad, Vic?'

'No fiddle! If Pete was up to his old tricks I knew nothing about it. If he had approached me I'd have shopped him and he'd have known that. And I wasn't sacked! And you can't bloody well prove otherwise!'

No, I couldn't. But I hoped to. I hoped the girl in the personnel office at the brewery came through for me.

'Why are you pestering me!' he snarled.

'You know why I'm in Saddlebridge, Vic. I'm after the bastard who killed my parents. So I'm looking for motives. You have one. You and dad did some thieving together at the brewery. Perhaps he tried to cheat you.'

'Motive!' He leaned forward; spittle splashed my face. 'If you want motives — try Sammy Kent — or your soft Uncle Frank.'

'Frank! Why should — ?'

'Hell!' he cut in. 'Everybody hated Pete! He was a snide and vicious bastard!'

He slammed the door in my face and that was just about that. My first interrogation had turned sour. But I had another name to work with — Sammy Kent.

It wasn't a large village, and it didn't take a great detective to find the detached cottage on the far side of the village from the Fox Inn, up the incline and close to the church. I asked a boy on a bicycle.

The gate squeaked as I pushed it open. The stones on the path were chipped and worn. I knocked on the door twice. No one answered. The drawn curtains puzzled me. I knocked once more then moved to the back. The garden stretched out, unkempt and empty, a large windowless garage at the bottom. I pushed my face to a chink in the curtains at the back of the house. Nothing. I was leaving when I noticed her.

She leaned on the wall that divided this cottage from hers, watching me. I smiled and approached her. I assured her I wasn't a housebreaker. She didn't respond. Her face showed no emotion. I guessed she knew who I was, but she gave no sign of recognition. I asked her about Sammy Kent. Her voice was flat and to the point.

'I don't know where he is or when he'll be back. He does odd jobs around the district. Sometimes he's gone for days at a time.'

It was obvious she wanted to know what business I had with her neighbour, but refrained from asking. I had no intention of enlightening her.

★ ★ ★

I spent another evening in the taproom, a stubborn glutton for punishment.

I parked myself on the same chair, by the same table. The faces around me were the same, and the atmosphere. Chilly might be the right word, icy more descriptive. I was again the man who sat alone.

Hanson was there. Occasionally I'd see his thumb jerk in my direction, notice the wide smirk on his face, hear the sniggering laughter. I was the butt of his humour, but I did nothing. There was nothing for me to do. I decided I would not be driven away.

It was around nine o'clock when he entered. A tall man, deeply tanned. He drew the others to him; the hub, the bringer of genuine smiles and laughter. He stood at the bar, talked animatedly while others listened. I studied him, intrigued. I wondered who he was. I was soon to find out.

He came out of the crowd, stood over me, then took a seat. He introduced himself as Robbie Sandford, and presumed that I was Jimmy. His handshake was warm and firm. He asked if I suffered from one of those social diseases he often read about in the Sunday papers. He laughed merrily. I was suddenly at ease.

Drily, I commented on the friendliness of the villagers.

'Take no notice.' He laughed out loud. 'They believe you have to have lived in the village at least twenty years to earn the right to sit in this room.'

He asked if my uncle had been in tonight. That startled me. I asked if Frank was a regular. He nodded. It usually took a broken leg to keep Frank away. That saddened me. Frank's absence could only be attributed to my presence. Robbie was asking if it was true that I was intent on solving the murders.

The way he said it brought a smile to my lips. It seemed foolish to me now. Myself, trying to solve a seventeen year old murder. I asked if I was making a fool of myself.

'I can't answer that for you.' His voice had turned serious. 'But personally, I would say it was best left alone. Many years have passed.'

Seventeen, I told myself. I didn't agree with him. And the time span was of little importance. The killer of my parents deserved to be caught, and punished.

I was suddenly resolute again. I asked if he had known my father.

He nodded, voice wistful. 'We were known as the inseparable four. Pete, myself, George Slater, and Dave Pearson.'

I sat up. I hadn't known Dave Pearson came from Saddlebridge, though I should have guessed. I was also surprised to learn that George Slater had been my father's friend.

'We were the same age,' Robbie was saying. 'You might say we grew up together, the four of us.'

I recalled something I was told in Penningstone. My father ran around with a gang that specialised in smashing up cafes and pubs. I asked if he and George had been part of that gang. His laughter filled the air.

'No. We drifted apart in our early teens. George and I stayed close to home. I worked on the farm, George helped his dad here at the Fox. Dave and Pete were free, and ranged further. They did get into a couple of scrapes, though chasing women seemed to be their major preoccupation. Then Pete married and moved to Penningstone. Dave already lived there, had done since he was sixteen. We hardly saw Dave again. It was different with Pete. He returned often. He was always close to his mother.'

We talked on until closing time. We touched on many subjects; from religion to politics, to the old films that were his passion. He invited me to visit his farm, and I promised to do so.

Sarah appeared, to take our glasses. She asked Robbie if he'd like to stay a little longer. He shook his head. Tomorrow was a busy day, and he needed his sleep.

He studied Sarah's retreating backside, smiled. He asked if I had sampled the delights of Sarah between the sheets. The question startled me. I feebly commented that I didn't think George would approve.

'Oh, as long as you don't make it too obvious George won't be minding. Sarah is a healthy young woman. You might be just what she needs to put the roses back in her cheeks.'

He stood, and I watched him leave. I followed a minute or so later, and there were still several drinkers at the bar. I had already learned that the taproom clique didn't trouble themselves with the licensing laws; membership was by invitation only. I wasn't invited.

My mood had lightened as I climbed the narrow staircase to my room. It didn't last. I stopped in my tracks. There was a chink of light showing under the door. My heart began to beat a little quicker as I slowly eased it open. 'You scared of the bogie man or something, sunshine!'

It was the voice of a stranger. I kicked open the door and stepped quickly inside. My fists were bunched.

'You are scaring the hell out of me, sunshine!'

The man sniggered loudly. He sat on the chair by the window. His rugged and bent face was thrown into sinister shadow by the overhead light. He couldn't have been much under sixty, his hair steel-grey. I guessed his height to be little above average, but he gave the impression of incredible power and bulk. His smile was sour, and the contempt in his eyes tangible.

'Who the hell are you!' I snapped, and knew my attempts at toughness were pathetic.

'I hear you have been looking for me. And I don't take kindly to itinerant scuffs peeping through my window.'

It clicked. Sammy Kent. His nosy neighbour had told him I had been to his cottage. I tried to relax, sat on the edge of the bed. I was confused. I didn't know what questions to ask. He understood, and it clearly amused him.

'Your daddy was a bastard, sunshine!' he said coldly. 'A gutless moron. He could use his prick — and that was all he ever was — a prick! And your mummy was probably little better. Only a whore with her brains between her legs would marry filth like Pete Ellis.' The man stood. 'If that's all you wanted to know — you have the truth.'

Stunned, I watched him stride to the door. Then the hate and rage welled inside. He was talking about my mother and father! I grabbed his arm and he

70

spun. He parried my punch with ease. The sickly grin on his face almost paralysed me. Too late, I realised I had been goaded into this attack. I didn't see the punch that slammed into my stomach. I was suddenly lifted, tossed across the room. The bed buckled under me. I was face down, gasping for air. His weight was on me and my arm was twisted up my back. My mouth opened in a scream of anguish but no sound came. My head was wrenched back by the hair.

'I thought you Aussies were tough nuts,' he mocked. 'But this is like wrestling a girl. I think I'll do what I did to your daddy. I messed up his face for a while. A month before he could even smile.'

He yanked my head back further. The blow exploded close to my ear. Bells exploded in my head. My struggles were ineffective.

'I think I'll start with your teeth, sunshine. But don't fret. There is a good dentist in Penningstone.'

I waited for the blow that didn't arrive.

The door had burst open.

'Leave him!' the voice spat. 'Leave him or by God I'll stand up in court and point the finger at you, Sammy Kent.'

The weight eased off me. He pulled me onto my back and glanced down. For a moment I wondered if he'd spit in my face. Then he turned and stormed from the room, feet pounding on the stairs.

I shook my head to clear the pain. I heard her coming closer. Humiliated, I couldn't meet her eye.

'He's a gorilla,' Sarah stated flatly. 'I've seen him reduce men twice your size to jibbering hulks.'

She brushed back my hair. I felt her fingers begin to explore. I winced.

'Not much blood, sweetheart,' she almost cooed. 'And under the hairline. It won't show.'

She left the room. I heard the splash of water. Then she was back. She dabbed at my head with a wet towel. Her breath was warm. The strange scent of her shrouded me.

I tried to take my mind off her,

72

anything. I asked why Sammy Kent had done this to me.

'Sammy left the village when he was a young man,' she said, concentrating on my face. 'He was a boxer. He wasn't famous or anything. He fought at fairs mainly. Then he returned. He had a son with him, but no wife. Apparently she had left him. Then it happened. Oh, over twenty years ago now. The reservoir down the valley. Summer. Sammy's son would be about ten. He was swimming, larking about in the water. Then he began to scream.

'Not many people about, kids mostly. Your father was there. Sammy believes he should have saved his son. Some said your father tried, others that he only went through the motions. The accounts were confused. But as your father couldn't swim, nobody attached much blame to him — except Sammy. Grief probably, and guilt. The reservoir was dangerous and clearly marked as such. There had been other accidents. And Sammy let the boy run wild. He beat up your father. Of course I don't remember any of this,

73

but I've heard the story repeated many times.'

'Did my father report this beating to the police?'

'No.' She shook her head and her hair brushed my cheek. 'We settle such differences amongst ourselves. The villagers got together and warned Sammy off. He never attacked Pete again, with his fists that is.' Her fingers touched my lips. 'Shall I stay awhile, sweetheart?'

'What about George?' But I didn't give a damn about George. My heart had begun to hammer. My hands had begun to roam and there was no turning back.

'He's nattering with his mates.' Her sharp tongue parted my lips. 'He'll be another hour at least.'

I swallowed her tongue.

6

'Not got any brighter with age,' grandmother said, tightening the bandage and stepping back to admire her work.

For the second time in under twelve hours I found myself at the mercy of a female who insisted on tending my wounds. Only grandmother's ministrations were less tender than Sarah's, and lacked that shattering climax.

I had woken in the early hours of morning, alone in my bed, but still with the feel of Sarah against my skin. I pondered on how easy it had been. Too easy for my peace of mind. She had been the huntress, I the victim. The pub lay quiet and still as I dressed and left.

As I expected, Uncle Frank was already busy in his garden. I picked up a spade and began to work alongside him. Too hard I worked. The blister didn't take long to form on my soft skin, and less time to burst. We didn't talk much. Every so often we'd pause and exchange a few words. I asked why he hadn't visited the Fox Inn since I'd booked in. He grinned sheepishly. I didn't need an explanation. It was scrawled across his face. I was an embarrassment. My presence placed him in a dilemma. Should he sit with me, his nephew, or his friends. I guessed Uncle Frank was never one for making decisions. Later, I brought Hanson into play. I repeated what Hanson had said, that Frank had a motive to kill his brother.

'I already said Pete and I didn't get along.' There was a flatness in his tone. 'Maybe Vic meant that. It was no secret. There was little brotherly love between us.'

I knew there was more, but I didn't press. A bit at a time was the way to deal with Frank. I worked on until I could grip the spade no longer. It had been a futile gesture. In my present state of fitness I was just incapable of grafting alongside men such as Frank. Grandmother brought me back to the present.

76

'When was the last time you held a spade?' she asked.

I didn't need to ponder on that question. I don't think I had ever held a spade in my life. And I seemed to be getting along with grandmother just fine, as long as I steered clear of more personal topics. When I touched on them her posture went rigid. But she was happy enough to recount village gossip, satisfy my itching curiosity.

'No mystery there,' she said. 'Betty Thomas. Married to a farmer over Penningstone way. He worked himself to death and she finished up with a farm that was barely worth a penny an acre. She sold it and went to work for Seth Slater, George's father. Her daughter Sarah would be five or six then. They lived in at the Fox, and whatever relationship Seth and Betty shared was between them and God. Betty was a sickly creature, whether real or imagined I wouldn't like to say, and soon took to her bed. Seth nursed her, and less charitable folk than myself reckoned she worked him to death the same as she had

77

her husband. And when Seth passed on, George took responsibility for her.'

I commented that it sounded strange to me. Why should George take responsibility? Grandmother puzzled on that.

'It concerned Sarah. In an odd way, George was to inherit Sarah. It was always accepted that they would marry. I never knew George to have a girlfriend. He was waiting for Sarah you see. As soon as Betty died they married.'

An interesting tale, but one that didn't get me very far in my search for a killer. I declined grandmother's offer of lunch. I said I had arranged to meet someone at the Fox Inn. A little frostiness returned to her manner.

'And behave yourself with Sarah,' she warned. 'She's a flighty one. And George Slater has a nasty temper on him when he's riled, especially if she is concerned.'

★ ★ ★

A little experiment in human nature; I slipped back into my role of journalist. A little time, a pleasant smile, and I found I wasn't quite the leper I thought I was.

The under-thirties and the over-seventies seemed to bear me no resentment, perhaps regarding me as something of a novelty, only the bulk of humanity in the middle. I stopped and chatted whenever the opportunity arose.

An elderly man in his garden — mind so crystal clear he could recall the events of seventy years ago as clearly as yesterday. A young woman pushing a pram — sharp of mind and eye, and certainly tongue. Two teenage girls sitting on a wall and watching the world drift by — desperate to be away from a place where nothing seemed to happen.

I had learned a little more of Saddle-bridge, and its inhabitants. I was still an alien, but at least some of my earlier paranoia had evaporated.

★ ★ ★

George behind the bar. He showered me with a glare that condemned me as a trouble-maker and he wished I'd take presence elsewhere. I didn't. I took a stool by the bar and scrupulously slopped my beer and spilled my peanuts. He constantly cleared the mess with rapid sweeps of his cloth.

I bumped into Sarah at the top of the stairs, a pile of linen over her arm. A small smile twitched the corners of her mouth. She commented that I had been a little rough on the sheets. I pressed her against the wall as she tried to squeeze past. The smile fled her face.

'George,' she mumbled, twisting free. I watched her move quickly around the bend in the stairs.

I wondered what the hell was happening. She hadn't seemed too concerned about George last night. But then, last night she knew where George was, and just now she probably didn't.

I decided to hell with Sarah. I kicked off my shoes and flopped on the bed. The next I knew I was awakening with a start. I had slept for three hours. I was soon on the move again.

★ ★ ★

The late afternoon had cooled. There was a touch of rain in the air. I tramped the path that led over the hill they referred to locally as the Peak. Saddlebridge lay below me, brooding in the grey light. To my right the valley wound away, cut by the stream that ran down to Penningstone, broadening many times before it reached the sea. To my left, more hills, green and purple, patched with small stone walls. I plodded on. My muscles began to ache again, the blister on my palm throbbed.

I don't know where she came from. One moment I was alone, the next she was standing on the path in front of me.

She was quite something. Her dark eyes were set in a wide and flawless face. She was tall and slender. Her long black hair whipped around in the breeze.

'Jimmy?' Her voice was light and pleasant.

I realised that I was staring, that she was growing disconcerted. I smiled, and it wasn't difficult. I was making some banal comment about her being the

81

best-looking girl I had ever laid eyes on. It was close to the truth.

'I'd like to think so.' She almost curtseyed.

Now it was her turn to examine me. She asked about the bandage on my hand. I told her. She decided grandmother was right. I wasn't very bright. We were talking and chiding each other like old friends; then a thought occurred to me.

'By the way,' I said. 'Just who are you?'

She was suddenly downcast. She even blushed. It turned out she was a certain Susan Smith, sixteen growing on seventeen, spinster of this parish, and the niece of Robbie Sandford. He had told her I might be calling at the farm. She presumed he had informed me he had a niece. She had decided to meet me half way, to act as escort.

We walked in companionable silence for a while, then she began to talk, chatter along merrily. We came around a corner and she pointed.

'The Sandford homestead,' she said in a voice tinged with pride.

It was no ranch. A farmhouse, white-washed out-buildings, a stone yard at the front and sides. I heard the flap of wings and the cluck of hens, and the rich smell of pigs caught my nostrils.

It was a pleasant evening, a hundred times more congenial than an evening spent at the Fox Inn. There was a radio, an old television on which I presumed Robbie watched his old movies. Books lined the walls, then spilled over to cover the furniture in happy confusion. They were, I discovered, a close and loving family.

There was Robbie, so easy to communicate with. His niece Susan, bubbly and attentive. Her parents Ben and Ruth Smith. Ben was a little taciturn, to put it mildly. He anchored himself in his comfortable chair, puffed on his pipe contentedly, his only contribution being to nod his head when directly addressed. He reminded me of Uncle Frank. Ruth was an attractive woman in her early forties. She smiled easily, possessed a great deal of her brother's charm, though lacked his conversational powers. And she cooked like a dream.

It was getting late when Susan suddenly left the room. She returned carrying a large leather album. She knelt by the side of my chair, and began to turn the pages.

'He isn't interested in those old photographs, Susan.'

There was a rough edge I would never have expected to hear in his voice. He obviously doted on the girl. My attention, and I guessed the others, turned to Robbie Sandford. There was a grim set to his jaw. I glanced down to the girl. She seemed puzzled and upset. Her voice matched.

'I only wanted to show Jimmy the photographs of Mum and Aunt Mary.'

Robbie's face softened. He smiled at the girl, then rose to his feet. He mumbled something about a farmer's work never being done. He had reached the door when he turned.

'Show Jimmy the photographs, Susan,' he said, then he closed the door behind him.

Susan did show me the photographs.

They began with two small toddlers in white dresses. She turned the pages slowly, often glancing into my face. The girls were twins, identical in dress and features. They progressed from childhood to adolescence, into womanhood. Susan seemed very proud to be the daughter of a twin.

Robbie hadn't returned when I decided it was time for me to leave. Ruth offered Ben's services to drive me back. He was relieved by my refusal, returning contentedly to suck on his pipe. Susan insisted she guide me. We paused as we approached the spot where we had met earlier. She asked what I thought of her family.

'I like them,' I answered truthfully. Then I had a question of my own. 'Why did Robbie get upset when you brought out the album?'

'Oh.' Her eyes rose to the dark sky. 'Aunt Mary. Mum and she were twins, only eleven months younger than Robbie himself, but I feel Mary was his favourite sister.'

'And Mary died?' I asked, jumping to

an obvious conclusion.

'Oh, no.' She swung around, eyes bright in the darkness. 'She went away, just after I was born. Nobody understands why. She just packed her bags and went. Robbie never heard from her again, not even a letter. I think that's what hurts him, not knowing what became of her.'

A strange emotion touched my heart. She was very sweet and very vulnerable. I smiled, brushed the hair from her face and kissed her forehead. We parted on the hillside, with my promise that I would visit the farm again.

I didn't walk far. I found a stone wall. I sat, enjoyed the night. Wispy clouds now rolled across the dark sky, sudden glimpses of twinkling stars in the heavens those millions of miles away. It felt good to be alive, to have my feet planted on this earth. I must have sat there at least three hours. I didn't trouble to check my watch.

There wasn't a single light in a single window as I approached the village. I was off the path and my feet made little noise on the tarmac of the lane. I experienced the urge to whistle, but somehow that seemed sacrilegious on a night such as this, when peace and tranquillity were all around. The world suddenly shattered.

The shot exploded behind and to my left, the air rushed above my head. I froze. The explosion hurled my mind backwards, deep into the blackness of the nightmare. There had been two explosions then, explosions that had snatched my parents from me. And now I stood on leaden feet. I waited for the second explosion, the pain. My limbs refused to function, project me away from here. The second explosion thundered in my ear, another rush of air above my head.

Then I ran. My arms pumped madly. I could have sworn I heard the cackle of insane laughter following me.

I covered the half mile to the Fox Inn in seconds, or so it seemed. The door was locked and I fumbled with the key Sarah had given me. I was inside, clanking home the bolts. No lights, no sound. I found the stairs and hurled myself up them. I threw myself on the bed. It took all my remaining courage not to bury my head under the blankets and curl into a ball.

Some bastard had tried to kill me! Some bastard had tried to end my life the same way he had my parents. With the blast of a shotgun! I wondered if it was the same gun that had taken those lives so long ago.

And why try to kill me!

Somebody was scared of me. Somebody was trying to stop me asking questions. Why? How close was I to the killer? What had I stumbled across since I arrived? Vic Hanson? Sammy Kent? They were the only names I could come up with.

I cringed at a noise on the landing. Then I recognised the footsteps. My lurching heart slowed. She knocked loudly, called my name. She entered the room and half closed the door. She came closer. A long dressing gown was corded at her waist. The scent of her filled the room, drifted into every corner, enveloped me. There was no expression on her face, only the provocative thrust of the hips.

'What has happened?' Her voice was unnaturally loud, and I realised it wasn't for my benefit. It was meant for George at the far end of the landing. 'It sounded like the devil himself was chasing you.'

The only light was that which filtered through the window. It cast shadows across her face, highlighting the lines and contours, yet strangely softening them. There was a serenity there, and that startled me.

'Somebody tried to kill me,' I said flatly, hoping for a reaction. I read nothing on her face. My voice rose. 'Somebody took two pot shots at me! Do you hear!'

'Calm yourself.' Her voice was still too loud, grating on my nerves. Her hand brushed my hair and I knocked it away. 'And don't be silly. If anyone around here had tried to kill you — you'd be dead.' The simplicity of her words chilled me. 'Probably youngsters larking about. They probably only intended to frighten you.'

Her hand came out again, fingers snaking into my hair. I caught her wrist and twisted it from me.

'Relax,' she cooed, voice barely audible now. Magically, her dressing gown fell open. 'Hurry. For God's sake hurry.'

I was falling back, responding to the urgency of her flesh, the pressure of her body on mine, her breath in my face, her lips and teeth bearing down.

It was over in seconds, and she was gone. I was left alone, mind in turmoil, lost and frightened.

7

It took less than ten minutes to locate the exact spot. The grass was trampled where he had stood and waited, but there was no further evidence of his having been there. No empty cartridge cases, no butt ends tossed carelessly aside, no nylon fibres clinging to the stone wall that would paint a vivid picture for a forensic expert.

I stood where he had stood. I leaned on my elbows as he had possibly done, sighted down an imaginary barrel, then softly pulled an imaginary trigger.

I straightened, allowed my mind to roam around the possibilities.

I agreed with Sarah on one point. If the gunman had meant to kill me — I'd be dead, and that knowledge sent a rush of relief racing through me. At a range of no more than ten yards, even at night, he could not have missed. He had deliberately aimed above my head.

And I was no expert on firearms, but surmised that the blast of a shotgun at this range would have blown chunks out of me.

On another point my opinion varied with Sarah's. I had been no victim of a kid larking about. Somebody had tried to scare the life out of me, to scare me away from Saddlebridge. Well, it hadn't worked. I was staying.

I wondered what would have happened if I hadn't run. What if I'd turned to face him? Would he have ducked down, evaded me as he surely could in the darkness? Possibly. Or possibly there might have been another result. I shuddered. I decided if I hadn't taken the course I had, though admittedly motivated by stark fear, I might now be lying on a mortuary slab.

* * *

There were few patrons in the saloon bar when I reached the Fox Inn. Sarah was behind the bar. We didn't speak, simply acknowledged each other with the barest of nods. I went off in search of George. The taproom stood empty. I eventually found him in the private sitting room, stretched out on the sofa, surrounded by the Sunday newspapers. He wasn't happy about my intrusion. The PRIVATE sign on the door meant exactly what it said. He didn't put his obvious thoughts into words.

'Taking it easy I see, sport?' I said brightly.

'Thanks to you I didn't get much sleep last night.' He turned a page noisily. 'A man's home isn't his bloody home these days.'

I wasn't about to be put off by his pearls of wisdom. I flopped on a chair and made myself comfortable. I asked who he thought had taken those shots at me. He grimly pretended I wasn't in the room. Silence greeted me. I recalled grandmother's warning. George possessed a fierce temper when roused. I wondered if I might be pressing too hard. But still, I repeated the question, and got the same result. Silence. My third attempt had a different effect. He balled up the newspaper and tossed it away. I had finally got under his skin.

'I'd say some bugger doesn't like you!' he rasped. 'And I'd say that bugger has taste. As to his identity — I couldn't say.'

'Like to congratulate him though, eh, sport?' I goaded.

'Congratulate him! I'd have congratulated him if he'd stuck the bloody thing up your backside and given you both barrels at once.'

That was plain enough, straight talking. And no play-acting from me now. My voice was deadly serious. 'What have you got against me, George?'

'You're scum!' The intensity of his hatred made me flinch. 'Arriving here out of nowhere. Dressed like a dosser yet driving a swank car, arse hanging out of the patches in your pants. Sport this, sport that. As if you're talking to a bloody serf. Well I'm no serf, squire! I'm twice the man you are — or ever will be! And if the truth were told — you are probably even less of a man than your dad!'

'Dad?' I tried to keep my voice

flat, devoid of the emotion that rose inside. 'I thought you and he were mates.' Some of the sarcasm slipped back into my voice. 'Members of the famous inseparable four.'

'Hell! Somebody is pulling your leg. He was just bearable when we were kids, so I endured him. But he never grew up. Acted the same at twenty as he did at ten! A cheeky kid with a smart and ready answer is one thing, good for a laugh, but when he's a man he should act like a man. Everything Pete saw he had to have, especially if it belonged to someone else.'

George was on his feet. The door slammed behind him, and I was left with my thoughts, more puzzled than ever. I decided on a trip to Penningstone.

★ ★ ★

Sergeant Cooper closed the filing cabinet and looked at me. I was lucky to find him here on a Sunday, unlucky to find him so busy. An accident on the bypass and a stream of football coaches had been diverted through Penningstone. Two coaches had stopped and their passengers had gone to war with the local hard-nuts. The cells were soon filled and the station was thrown into chaos.

'I thought you wanted to snoop around on your own,' he said. 'Get the feel of the thing?'

I shrugged. 'Now I have the feel. According to you, Charlie Grey hinted that he knew the identity of the killer. Do you know who he had in mind?'

'Not a clue,' he replied impatiently. 'He certainly didn't confide in me. And it was no more than a hint. And I think I made that perfectly clear the last time we spoke.'

I ignored the censure. I had to start somewhere. 'But you worked on the case. Maybe he concentrated on one man more than the others.'

'If he did, nobody noticed.' There was a snap in his voice, then he sighed. 'Look. I was young and green at the time, and Charlie was almost God. So perhaps I gave you the wrong impression. Charlie was as fallible as the next man.

He made mistakes. He was good. He earned his reputation. But he was not one of those super detectives you read about in comics.'

That was reasonable enough. 'Is it possible he wrote something down?'

'Charlie wasn't one for writing.' He laughed. 'There are the official statements of course, the general outline the investigation took until the big boys moved in and shunted us out, but little more.' He shrugged. 'Charlie was a loner. When he had his teeth into something he'd see it through alone, fag between his lips and whisky flask in his pocket. He'd talk to people, nag away until he got something he could use. Nothing on paper, no sidekick at his heels.'

His little speech over he slipped behind his desk. 'Okay, when I have the time I'll skim through the reports to refresh my memory. Perhaps something might occur to me. I take it the reason you are here is because you are getting nowhere?'

I tried to detect a hint of smugness in his tone, but found none.

'I've kicked over a few stones and

made myself unpopular,' I told him. 'Otherwise — nothing.'

That wasn't quite true, but for the moment I wished the information to flow in one direction — from him to me.

'Right.' He spread his hands in apology. 'You can see how it is at the moment. But I will go through the files. I'll phone you and we can get together. Possibly over a couple of jars?'

That sounded fine to me, and I left him to help sort out the chaos.

★ ★ ★

'If I don't talk I've an idea that you might just decide to haunt me.'

'I'm stubborn,' I admitted, and Dave Pearson managed a reluctant smile. We found an almost quiet corner in a pub crowded with lunch-time drinkers.

'We were guilty right enough,' Dave was saying. 'Five jobs if I remember right. Places with no burglar alarms, and we nicked only cash. We'd already had our fingers burned when we took goods, so we steered clear of anything that had to

98

be sold later. Petty stuff.' He examined his glass dolefully. 'And that is how I feel about it now — petty. We were cheap berks. I regret what we did. Anyway, the bogies pulled us in, along with others with previous form. They had no real evidence so they released us. We pulled one more job from sheer bravado, then called it a day. And that is the story of our life of crime. Pretty pathetic wouldn't you say?'

It wasn't my place to judge. At least Dave regretted the past, and I hoped my father would have done the same if he'd lived. Somehow I doubted it. Again I asked for information concerning my father and Vic Hanson.

'I already told you,' Dave answered. 'Pete hinted that he and Hanson were working a fiddle at the brewery. He'd been drinking so I took it with a pinch of salt. It seemed unlikely to me. You have to understand the character of Hanson. Always Mr Clean, prided himself on his honesty. When we were kids he once shopped us for nicking apples. His conscience wouldn't allow him to do otherwise. He loved uniforms. He wanted to be a policeman but couldn't make the height. The fire brigade turned him down. With the job at the brewery he found paradise, and a uniform; the rumour is he slept in it. It was only when I heard a whisper that Hanson had got the boot for thieving that I began to wonder if Pete hadn't given me the truth that night.'

We went into it further, but there was little more he could add. I asked why my father returned to Saddlebridge so often.

'Saddlebridge was a magnet to him.' Dave waited while the barmaid changed the glasses. 'He was close to his mother. But that wasn't the main reason. You see, Saddlebridge didn't like Pete. He shouted his mouth off too often, and too freely. He always said and did the wrong thing, though quite deliberately. I'll not lie to you. Pete was a stirrer, and a devil when he had a gutful of ale.'

It sounded a good reason for steering clear of Saddlebridge. It sounded as if Dave had got his reasoning mixed up. I pointed this out to him.

'I know,' he said. 'But it was sheer perversity. Hurt Pete, sting him, and he had to go back for more until he decided he had won. I guess he never beat Saddlebridge. Pete was my mate, but a more awkward customer you never met. I didn't get along with Saddlebridge either. You couldn't sneeze without everybody in the village catching cold. But I had the sense to clear out, and stay out.'

I told him that in some quarters, even after seventeen years, the hatred towards my father was still tangible. He wasn't surprised, commented that Saddlebridge never forgot of forgave. I went a little deeper, delved into the personalities of some of the characters I had met.

'I can't help you there,' he said. 'Sure enough, as kids we knocked around together. Pete, George, myself, and Robbie. But we were never quite the friends you imply. Robbie was practically running the farm before he left school, those twins forever at his heels. As for George — if there was ever any particular animosity towards Pete on his part, I knew nothing of it.'

I brought him around to the night of the murders.

'I had arranged to meet Pete in this very pub,' he said. 'He didn't show and I thought no more of it. It wasn't unusual. I decided he'd changed his mind. Next thing I know he's dead. The police woke me up and took me to the station. Charlie Grey himself. He hammered away at me about the robberies, but I stayed mute on that score. Then Charlie switched tactics. One question in particular. Did Pete have enemies? Well, there was plenty that didn't like him, but I knew of none that would take a shotgun to him. He had a couple of girlfriends, one married, and I suppose they cleared the husband. That was it.'

'And Grey switched his attention to Saddlebridge?'

'So I believe. Then they chucked him off the case. Old Charlie died not long after.'

'Who do you think killed my father, Dave?'

He took a long pull on his drink. 'Mate, I haven't the slightest idea.'

I told him if he remembered anything that might be important to give me a ring at the Fox Inn.

* * *

I was soon back in Livingstone Terrace talking to Mrs Parkinson. I asked who owned number fifteen, if it had been occupied since the murders. Her forehead furrowed in a frown.

'No,' she said. 'It has been empty since that night. The children in the street used to pretend it was haunted. Touch the door and run away, that sort of thing.' She peered at me closely. 'And I presumed you knew. The house belongs to your grandmother.'

That was a stunner. I asked since when.

'Since the day your parents moved in. Jenny herself told me. She said she paid rent to her mother-in-law. And she comes back you know — your grandmother. Three or four times a year.' Mrs Parkinson frowned again. 'I hear her arrive. Sometimes I see her. She stays two hours or so, then leaves.'

Oh, Christ. What the hell was grandmother playing at! What did she do inside that house? My mind whirled as I walked away.

There was some activity at the brewery as I drove past, but I presumed the office staff were not on duty. Anyway, the girl had said next week, and tomorrow was next week.

* * *

'You make it sound as if I'm doing something dirty!'

Well, I certainly didn't think it normal. But I kept my thoughts to myself. Grandmother stood over me. Shades of the grandmother I remembered from all those years ago came back to my mind. I shivered. She stalked across the room, stalked back. Then my own temper snapped.

'For the love of God!' I yelled. 'Stop feeling sorry for yourself! Don't have me hating you again, grandmother!'

To my astonishment she stilled. Her eyes met mine for only a second, but for the first time in our lives I think we understood each other. She sat meekly.

'It is my house,' she said quietly. 'I can do whatever I like with it. And it is easier there. So quiet and still. I can remember more clearly.' Her eyes locked on mine fiercely. 'I talk to him you know. I talk to Pete. And he listens. If that makes me a madwoman — so be it.'

I wondered if she was mad. Just a little, I decided, but far from insane. I could have mentioned that she might ask her son who killed him the next time she spoke to him. But such bitter sarcasm was best left in the mind. And strangely, I experienced the urge to comfort her, yet I stayed my distance. She hadn't finished.

'And you. You were never a prisoner in this house. You have twisted everything. Except for school, you refused to leave the front door. Your room, the kitchen, the back garden, that was all you seemed to want. I knew you were unhappy, but I could do nothing for you.'

She could have ceased to slap my face, ceased to pour scorn on the mother I never knew. She could have done that for me. But it was impossible to hate her now. And was it true? Had I twisted everything? Perhaps. My memory had surely played tricks. I found I liked her. Almost angrily I had to swallow emotions that were reaching towards love. I asked for the key to the house in Livingstone Terrace, and she handed it over without a murmur. There was much more she wanted to reveal, but for now the emotions had to stay locked inside.

'Do you know who murdered them, grandmother?' I asked in a voice that barely reached a whisper.

'Somebody in Saddlebridge,' she croaked. 'That's what the policeman kept saying. The one who smelled of musty bread. He kept on at me, looking out of the window towards you as you stood in the garden with Frank. He took me way back into the past, almost to the time Pete was barely able to walk. Pete was high-spirited you know. Often got into bits of trouble, but there was no

106

harm in him, no malice.'

She wasn't fooling me, and I wondered if she was fooling herself. One thing I had come to accept, my dad was a bit of a bastard, whichever way you looked at it. But grandmother's eyes had misted.

'Little more than give a dog a bad name. Anything that happened — and he was the one the accusing finger pointed at. He made me tell it all, that policeman. I don't think I was able to help him. I knew of no one who would want to harm Pete.'

'Sammy Kent?' I put forward.

'Oh, him.' She wiped a hand across her eyes. 'That is an example. Pete couldn't swim, yet that man as good as accused him of letting his son drown. How could he do that? He beat Pete up, but I put a stop to that. I went to see Mr. Sammy Kent. I warned him that if he ever laid a hand on my son again I'd push a bread knife into his black heart. He didn't touch Pete again.'

A slightly different version from Sarah's. I found myself believing grandmother.

'But I don't think he had anything to

do with Pete's death,' she said absently. 'It was years after his son drowned. And if the murderer really did live in Saddlebridge, the police would have caught him, wouldn't they?'

Which contradicted my presence in Saddlebridge. But maybe so, and maybe not. And her naivete was touching. I left her then. I had removed more shadows from my past.

8

I decided to give the taproom a miss. My resistance to silence was getting low. And just one snigger from Vic Hanson in my direction and I was in the mood to shove my fist down his throat. I opted for the saloon bar.

Lesley was on duty. She introduced me to a young man she claimed to be her boyfriend, though he didn't seem to be too sure about this.

He was the son of a farmer and very interested in Australia, especially Australian sheep. He had picked up the notion that all Australians were experts on this subject. I wasn't. But we talked, and I spouted a lot of gibberish. Then Sarah appeared and whispered in my ear. I followed her out. I found Uncle Frank waiting in the passage. He opened his jacket to reveal a whisky bottle and two glasses. He grinned and slapped me on the shoulder. We moved upstairs to my room.

I took the bed. He shuffled about, commented that he had never been up here, that it was nice and cosy. It was some time before he finally decided to take the chair by the window. He crossed and uncrossed his legs. I wondered why he was behaving like a flustered virgin. I spluttered on the whisky. His own slipped easily down his throat and he refilled his glass. I told him about the house in Livingstone Terrace, and grandmother's visits. He already knew.

'She bought the house when they married,' he said. He filled his glass again, spilled a little. 'I know she goes there.' His voice fell to a sly whisper. 'She used to attend seances. Did you know that?' I didn't. I shook my head. 'The whole bit. Mediums wailing, lights flickering, communing with the dead. She thinks it's a secret, but it isn't. Weird, I'd call it.'

Perhaps. But many intelligent people believed in the spirit world; I'd spoken to a few, so who was I to judge?

And Uncle Frank talked on as I had never heard him talk before. It struck me that it was the whisky loosening his tongue. The bottle was soon half empty, and I still had the dregs in my first glass. He had long since ceased to offer me a refill. I lay back and allowed his words to wash around me. He was getting something off his chest and only my presence was required, not my opinions. I heard George shout 'time' somewhere below, voices at the front door. Soon after, Sarah's feet sounded on the stairs and paused outside the door. A short rap and it opened. Her head popped round. She wished us a cheerful goodnight and the door closed.

'He was mother's pet,' Frank was repeating, voice a little slurred. 'That's why I hated him. I loved her and she showed me nothing. But him! He would steal from her and blame me — and she'd believe him. It was me that had to go without supper. Nothing changed, even when he married. Always coming back, always crying on her shoulder.' Frank's fist hit the palm of his hand with a loud crack. 'Came here a lot — the Fox. Tossed his money about like there was no tomorrow, insisted on buying the rounds as if we were penniless yokels. Stirred up trouble. If anybody had a weak spot Pete soon sniffed it out — stuck the knife in and twisted. But you could never get through to him. So bloody insensitive you wouldn't believe!'

His words grew more scrambled, then almost indecipherable. He finally lurched to his feet. His feet clomped unsteadily on the stairs.

I closed my eyes, rested. I think I dozed for a few minutes. Then there were voices in the passage below. The bolts clanked shut on the door. The voices came from outside now. Loud and raucous, much laughter. Feet munched on the gravel car-park but no engine kicked into life. I heard George on the stairs, move past my door. No Sarah tonight. I slept alone. I didn't even trouble to take my clothes off.

★ ★ ★

Bastards! Peevish bastards!

I now saw the cause of the merriment

outside the pub last night, and the crunch of feet on the gravel while no car drove away. The bastards had tipped a tin of whitewash over the bonnet of my car. I felt sick, and angry.

I was soon aware that George had followed me out. I turned. For the first time I saw something that resembled a smile on his face.

'I don't suppose there is any point in asking who was the last to leave the pub last night, sport?'

The almost smile stretched into a leer. 'Don't rightly recall — squire.'

'You just supplied the whitewash, sport.' I lashed out at the empty tin and sent it spinning across the gravel. 'Is that the truth of it?'

'Supplied nobody with nothing — squire.' With that he retreated back inside the pub.

I spent a gruelling half hour with a mop and bucket, and at last the car was restored to something like its former glory. I had washed and reached my room when Sarah shouted from below. Somebody on the phone. I took the call in the office. I expected to hear the voice of Sergeant Cooper. I didn't. Larry Jenkins from the newspaper barked down the line.

'A bit of a coincidence has occurred that might blow you a bit of good, chum,' he was saying. 'She popped in out of the blue. Visiting relatives in the area and came over to the office to see how the peasants were managing without her.'

I hadn't a clue what he was talking about, or the identity of the mysterious her. I asked him to explain.

'Bit slow this morning, chum,' he said cheerfully.

I had a hang-over, some clowns had whitewashed my car. So what the hell was he expecting? And how the hell did he know where to find me?

'The nose of an experienced journalist,' he explained insufficiently. 'And you remember — fancy knickers who went to work in television.' It dawned. The reporter who had come to this village last year on much the same mission as myself. 'Naturally I had to mention your visit. Lucky I did. Seems she did unearth something that was new. Seems your father was at the Fox Inn three days before he died. The Sunday night — quite late. There happened to be a punch-up, and he was involved.'

Moving at last. I liked what I was hearing. I asked for more details.

'Hold on,' he cautioned. 'That is more or less it. Your father was there and got into a fight. No more details. Fancy knickers got the information from a Vic Hanson and that little snippet cost her a bruised backside, and even she was prepared to go no further in the cause of truth and justice. So that's it. Thought you would want to know. The snippet was not included in the published article because Hanson later denied it. Keep in touch, chum.'

He had hung up before I could thank him.

* * *

I found Robbie Sandford behind the farmhouse. He sensed my approach and turned. He smiled, turned back to the direction he had been looking. I followed his eyes.

It was a small garden enclosed by a white picket fence, fringed by bushes, a small rockery in one corner; the whole affair was no more than twelve feet by twelve.

'You should see it in Spring,' he said. 'The flowers. A violent splash of colour you can see for miles. This is my beacon.'

There was an intensity in his voice, yet a great distance. It disturbed me. I tried to lighten the mood. I commented that I wouldn't have thought a farmer would have much time for such a frippery.

My words seemed to sting, but he recovered. He said quietly, 'There is always time for this.'

I told him about the gunshots fired above my head. He already knew. I gave him my theory on why it had happened. He demurred from offering an opinion. He hadn't visited the Fox Inn since the night he met me, and he hadn't heard that whitewash had been tipped over my car last night. He listened, then shook his head sadly.

'You have to try and understand how it was, Jimmy. They were dead, your parents, and we mourned them, but our trials were beginning. The police came. Then the reporters followed like a storm of locusts. To this day they still arrive. And there was one policeman in particular — Detective Chief Inspector Grey.

'He decided the murderer lived amongst us, in Saddlebridge. He made no pretence. He gave his opinion to everyone and anyone. He seemed to be everywhere, talking quietly yet nagging away at your mind, arousing anger where none should have been. Well, you can imagine the effect it had. You looked at your neighbour and began to wonder. Can my neighbour possibly be the killer? And you wondered if he was thinking the same about you. It was a bad time in such a small community.

'I, and many others, were in the Fox Inn at the time the murders took place — impossible for us to be

117

involved in Pete's death. And this is a farming community, many shotguns. The police examined them, gave them back, apparently satisfied, but that wasn't good enough for Grey. He continued to harass us.

'He was taken off the case, yet still he persisted. We held a meeting in the church hall, decided to complain to the authorities. It had little effect. He returned time and time again. Then he died in a car crash.

'That is why you are resented, Jimmy. You are stirring up old memories, old suspicions. You will have noticed that the young bear no animosity towards you. It is those who remember the dark period after the murders.'

I had worked all this out for myself some time ago. But I felt no regret, offered no apologies. I didn't give a damn what old suspicions I aroused. Saddlebridge could stew on its suspicions. I was doing what Charlie Grey had done before me — smoking out a killer. I meant to have the bastard who murdered my parents!

118

I pondered on what I had learned from Larry Jenkins earlier, wondered if I should ask Robbie if he knew anything about the fight that had occurred in the Fox Inn the Sunday before the murders, providing the information was correct and the fight actually took place. I decided to sit on it a while, work out the best way of using it. But I had one question, hard and to the point.

'Who do you think killed them, Robbie?'

He sighed. 'I really don't know. But no one from Saddlebridge. I'm sure of that. That policeman was wrong. Why they died I couldn't say. A jealous husband or boyfriend?' He studied the small garden. 'Pete was always playing around with the girls. There can be no hiding from that, Jimmy.'

I wasn't hiding from anything. And he was wrong. The killer lived in Saddlebridge. I knew that from deep inside my bones. I was as certain as old Charlie Grey before me had been.

★ ★ ★

I spotted her the exact moment she spotted me. The wind scattered her hair about her face and she constantly pulled it free, a leather case hung casually over her shoulder. She reminded me of a young heroine I had once seen on the cover of one of cousin Sal's romantic magazines. I pulled the car to a halt and stepped out, leaned on the bonnet. Susan smiled brightly. She asked if I had been to the farm.

I nodded. I recounted some of my conversation with Robbie. I asked what she was doing out of school so early. She grinned. She had feigned a headache, too pleasant a day to sit in a stuffy classroom.

She chattered on. She was studying for her 'A' levels, hoping her results would be sufficient to earn her a university place. I enquired after her ambitions.

'I can't make up my mind. Either a doctor or a housewife.' She grinned again, seemed terribly young. 'It is one great decision to make, isn't it? I think I'll plump for housewife. Ten children, that's what I'd like. Five sets of twins as you might already have guessed.'

It sounded a harder life than that of a doctor to me. We talked in this manner for a while, teasing. Then I asked about Robbie and his garden.

'Oh, that.' Some of the fun left her voice. Her face became serious. 'The garden has been there as long as I remember. It's somewhere for him to retreat to. To Robbie the garden is a very private sanctuary. He leans on the fence for hours. I don't know what goes through his mind, and I don't ask, or intrude on his thoughts. The other night when I brought out the album, that is where he went, why we didn't disturb him to say you were leaving.'

I found this interesting. I asked why Robbie had never married. She brightened.

'I don't really know. I often used to tease him, called him a crusty old bachelor. He only gave me the stock answers. He had never met Miss Right, the girls he fancied were already married, he never had the time. Suchlike.'

I didn't drive away immediately. I

watched her in the mirror. I smiled, decided she looked as delightful from the rear as she did from the front. Then she was gone and a strange emotion touched my heart, almost love, but perhaps not, perhaps no more than a yearning for innocence. I ceased daydreaming and plunged the car into gear.

* * *

There was no male voice bellowing from behind the closed door, but the telephone still insisted on clattering every few seconds. She sat behind the desk a little primly, and briskly flipped over the pages of the notepad. Her face was still far from pretty, but still quite fetching.

'Right, I did check,' she said. 'Your father. He was employed by this company for five years.' She rattled off the dates and I went through the motions of jotting them down. 'A good record, though his timekeeping was a little erratic.'

She looked up, eyed me. It was now apparent she knew exactly who I was, that my father had been murdered and the story I had given her about writing a history of my family was not true — and it intrigued her. I didn't attempt to enlighten her. I asked about Vic Hanson.

'That is different. And you might not like that.' From her tone I was sure I would like it very much. She went on, 'He was employed for some eleven years. Again, a good record. He was a security guard. Usually on the gate, checked what was entering and leaving the premises. But his record didn't stay clean. Almost sixteen years ago to this day, someone in accounts spotted a discrepancy. There was an internal investigation and Hanson came under scrutiny. Apparently, putting it simply, more barrels left the place than were actually paid for. It was never discovered how long this had been going on, or how much money was involved, but certainly it must have amounted to quite a tidy sum. Hanson, three drivers, and a checker in despatch were involved.'

'Were the police brought in?'

'No. Under the circumstances that

prevailed at the time that would not have been very diplomatic. Union problems. The unions claimed that any prosecution would be regarded as a slur on the entire workforce. In their wisdom the management agreed. The five men were quietly allowed to resign. A loophole in procedure had been plugged and that seemed to satisfy everybody.'

So Dave Pearson had been right. Hanson was a thief. I wondered how much he made from the fiddle.

I stood, glanced down at her hand and noted the absence of rings. I took a long look at her, decided I liked her, decided she reciprocated, and she was itching to know the truth behind my being here. And at the moment I didn't fancy Saddlebridge one little bit. I asked what time she finished. Half past six. I asked if she'd like a night out. She examined me, shrugged. I told her I'd wait in the car-park. If she wasn't interested she could keep on walking, if she was, to duck inside the car.

9

She ducked inside the car, as I knew she would.

If you didn't fancy a weeny-bopper disco, a beer at the local Labour Club, or a game of bingo, there wasn't a lot to do in Penningstone.

We settled for a quiet restaurant just outside town; an acceptable meal and a comfortable lounge bar, ending the night at her flat. I stayed less than an hour.

It had been a pleasant interlude, but now I was back to the brooding of Saddlebridge. The Fox Inn lay quiet but for the voices coming from the taproom at the far end of the passage. I moved quietly to the stairs and my room.

Second sight?

I don't know. Maybe a whiff on the air, something that didn't belong. Or more likely, though it didn't occur to me until later, the total blackness of the room. I hadn't closed the curtains before I left. But I was groping for the light switch when I suddenly ducked. Something swished over my head. I kicked out in the darkness. My toe connected. There was a grunt of startled pain. I followed up with my left fist, met no resistance other than parting air. My turn to grunt. The blow caught my ribs. His eyes were more accustomed to the dark. I was losing. My feet went from under me and I crashed to the floor with a dull thud. I waited for the pain of a boot smashing into my flesh. It didn't materialise. The door closed quietly, feet pattered on the stairs.

Groggily, I used the bed to pull myself upright. I took deep breaths. I swallowed the bile that rose to my throat. My breathing slowed.

Feet on the landing! Her feet! The door opened, the snap of a switch, and light flooded the room. I shaded my eyes to protect them from the glare.

'What is all the thumping about?'

Sarah stood in the doorway, hands on hips, night-gown corded at the waist, eyes skimming around the room.

126

'Who the hell was it!' I snapped.

Her face showed nothing. 'What are you talking about?'

'Where is the bastard who just ran from this room?'

Her face began to swim a little through my blurred vision. She tossed her head impatiently.

'I was in bed and something startled me. A thump, something crashing to the floor.' She came closer and leaned forward. Her nose wrinkled in disgust. I noted the rage on her face. 'You've been with a whore! You stink of her!'

'Stuff it! You sanctimonious bitch!' I was on my feet, still unsteady. She caught my elbow to stop me falling. 'Now where the hell is he?'

She stepped back. 'You're drunk. You've been drinking — and whoring! Nobody attacked you. Look at you! You can barely stand upright.'

'You must have heard him on the stairs!' But had she? The man had made little noise. She continued to stare at me as if I'd crawled out from a sewer. I resisted the urge to slap that

127

contemptuous look from her face. 'You heard him, you bitch!'

I pushed past her. Down the stairs and into the icy cool of the passage. I threw open doors as I went. Nothing. Finally, I kicked open the door to the taproom. I might not have existed. Not a single eye turned my way. Three of them. George, Vic Hanson, Sammy Kent. They sat around a table, concentrated on the cards in their hands.

'Which of you bastards was it!' I hoped my voice carried some authority, but I had the sickly idea it was little more than a girlish whine. It always rose uncontrollably when I was excited or angry.

'You want something, squire?' George asked without looking up. 'Some dastardly swine nicked your teddy bear?'

Oh, Christ. I was making a fool of myself again.

'No, sport. Teddy is tucked up asleep.' I had tried to bring some humour into my voice, failed. 'I just got back. There was somebody in my room. He attacked me. He ran down the stairs. He didn't leave by the front door, or I'd have heard him. He isn't in any of the other rooms. He couldn't have left by the back door because it's bolted on the inside, which leaves you three.'

'Perhaps he flew up the chimney,' Hanson piped, grinning at the healthy laughter that greeted his wit. But at least I now had the attention of all three men.

'He's drunk!'

Startled, I spun. Sarah had entered the room behind me. She took the posture that had become so familiar. Arms folded under her breasts, weight on one leg, hips thrusting. Her eyes were fixed on me, unblinking.

'Drunk as a lord,' she said coldly, voice addressing the men at the table, but meant for me. 'And he's been with a whore. You can smell the stink of her on him.'

'A real chip off the old block.' Sammy Kent spoke for the first time. 'I wonder if he's as prolific as his old man.'

My eyes swept around them. Each smiled in their own way: George mocking,

Hanson unable or unwilling to disguise his snigger, Kent wrathful with righteous hate, Sarah filled with controlled rage. And I recognised that all these people, with the possible exception of Sarah, saw me as an enemy, a threat, as potent as if I carried a loaded machine gun.

But what was I to do right now? Join them in a battle of wits and words? Impossible. Beat the truth out of them? Ridiculous. Ask them to roll up their trouser legs to see which carried the mark of my toecap on his shin? Laughable. No, I took a deep breath, swallowed my anger, turned and walked from the room. As I reached the stairs I heard the sudden roar of laughter. I gritted my teeth, and knew the real meaning of cold and blind hatred.

* * *

The nightmare chose that night to return. I awoke in a sweat, trembling. It took some time for me to regain control. I was exhausted but made no attempt to sleep again. Too scared, too terrified.

130

In the early hours I crept downstairs. From the machine I bought a pack of cigarettes, smoked my first cigarette in years, coughed on the smoke. It tasted foul. The second was better. With the third it was as though I had never given up. I did a lot of thinking but reached no concrete conclusions. I pondered on whether I should leave the Fox Inn and move in with grandmother. I decided against. There were answers to be found here, possibly the key to the whole mystery. And George resented my presence, so why hadn't he ordered me to pack my bags and get out? I had no answer.

And now the sun shone, and the only darkness in the world was in my own heart and mind. And even now I was unable to relax in this glorious morning. He blocked my path as I crossed the road from the Fox Inn. I stepped this way, and he stepped in front. I stepped there, and again he ended up in front of me.

'Are we going to tango all day,' I said wearily. 'Or are you going to spit out what you want?'

'I don't like scum accusing me of skulking about in the dark.' Sammy Kent rocked back on his heels. 'I do my fighting in the daylight. Nobody accuses me of being yellow.'

And he wasn't joking. He was doing one hell of a good impersonation of the villain in a cheap Western. And he was ready to take me on. Right here on the main road that passed through the centre of Saddlebridge.

'Oh, I know now that it wasn't you, Sammy,' I said. I even summoned a weak smile. 'I've had all night to ponder on it. The smell you see. He didn't have that peculiar stench of rotting flesh.'

I tensed. I waited for him to attack. In a strange way I wanted it to happen. One blow, that was all I asked for. One blow into that fat, ugly mouth and I'd gladly have taken a beating. But he wasn't ready. And I suddenly realised why. I was supposed to run. I was supposed to turn and run from this mindless thug! Well, it would snow in August before that happened.

'Fighting words,' he said, and there

was a new edge to his voice. I had got through. 'I ought to pull down your pants and smack your bum.'

'So that's what turns you on, Sammy?' Now I was doing the goading, and I enjoyed the feeling. 'I always suspected there was something a little effeminate about you.'

Oh, Christ. He was on the verge. I wondered if his brains had been scrambled in the boxing ring. His ugly face turned a deep purple. He almost walked through and over me. His shoulder on mine spun me, but he didn't glance back as he strode away.

★ ★ ★

'Who told you this!'

Vic Hanson kept me on the doorstep again, a pathetic little wretch of a man in his oversized pyjamas.

'And a lie,' he announced for the third time. 'I got bored with the job and jacked.'

'Last time it was because you found a

better job sweeping floors,' I commented drily, then smiled. 'A bit of a difference there, Vic. I can give you the dates, the men involved. The company allowed you to resign to avoid a tricky situation with the unions. It's all on the files, Vic. In black and white.'

He looked this way and that, like a cornered rat trying to find an escape route.

'Perhaps they got the wrong man,' he offered weakly.

'Balls. And before my father died he was part of your team. I think he tried to cheat you. From what I've learned that was his style. I think you decided to teach him a lesson. You went to the house and knocked on the door. I don't think you meant to kill him, just scare him with the gun, show him he wasn't meddling with rubbish. I think he tried to grab the gun and it went off accidently. Then my mother appeared. That stunned you. She wasn't supposed to be there. But you couldn't leave a witness. She had to die also.'

'You think! You think! You think a

lot, but you know nothing!'

He leaned closer, face twisted. 'You're a raggedyarsed clown, an imbecile. Part of my team! I wouldn't have anything to do with Pete Ellis, and he knew it. Blackmailing bastard! He fixed me with her! He got her to lead me on!'

I wanted to interrupt, question him, but that would have got me nowhere. I let his tirade run on.

'He blackmailed me! I was in, whether I liked it or not. And I made nothing! He didn't even offer me a share. Not that I would ever take a penny of stolen money. Then he died. Was I happy! I danced and sang when I heard. But even then I couldn't get out. The weasel in despatch, the other drivers. I could have had money then, a fair share, but I refused. Whatever happened I would still have my self-respect. Nobody could ever call me a thief. But they were children without Pete. Too greedy. Not satisfied with a few quid a week. It had to end. And did. We wcre lucky they didn't prosecute. So even dead, that bastard Pete did for me.'

It began to make sense. Hanson wasn't a willing member of the thieving ring. He had been coerced by my father, blackmailed into helping.

'What did he have on you, Vic?' I asked.

As soon as I opened my mouth the spell was broken, as I thought it might be. He had said just enough to justify his actions, and he knew it. His head shook grimly.

'You can go to hell!' he snapped.

'One thing, Vic. Go near my car again and I'll break your scrawny neck!'

'I'm not scared of you.' He stood to his full height. 'Blubbering like a great baby you were last night. No, I'm not scared of you.'

And I recognised that he wasn't, physically at least, but in other matters he certainly was. I checked my temper. 'And I suppose it wasn't you in my room, Vic?'

'There was nobody in your room.'

'He was there all right. But no, it couldn't have been you. He was man sized.'

'Go to hell!'
The door slammed in my face.

★ ★ ★

'It's hazy.' Uncle Frank grinned sheepishly. 'After I left you I did go back to the taproom for a few minutes. I don't recall much. I was drunk.'

That point I recalled clearly. I told him how whitewash had been splashed over my car.

'You think I'd do that?' he asked, facing me.

I shrugged. 'I just wondered,' I said absently. 'And like you said — you were drunk.'

'Drunk or sober — I wouldn't do that.'

I wasn't sure if I believed him. And why had he come to my room that night? Like a naughty schoolboy fulfilling a distasteful errand. And why did he need the whisky to give him the courage to talk to me? I began to wonder if there was anybody I could trust. I recalled the time I had spent here as a boy. I hated grandmother then; now I found myself almost loving her. I had loved Frank then, and now I didn't know what my feelings were towards him. Was he really the man I remembered? The man in whose quiet presence I found comfort? Now there was an evasiveness about him for which I could find no reasonable explanation, and a reluctance on his part to allow me the merest glimpse behind the incompetent mask he showed the world. And even now, I began to wonder if he had been as drunk as he seemed when he sat in my room. I changed the subject. I asked if he had visited the Fox Inn last night. It brought the sheepish grin back to his face.

'I decided to give it a miss,' he said. 'I drank more than my fair share the night before.'

I told him I had been attacked in my room; how his friends in the taproom had greeted my claim.

'Perhaps they were right, Jimmy,' he said thoughtfully. 'Perhaps you were drunk.'

It seemed Uncle Frank's loyalties lay

with his mates, not me. And despite my earlier thoughts — it still stung. I asked a more important question.

'The Sunday before he died — dad was at the Fox Inn — were you there?'

He muttered that it was likely, but he couldn't rightly remember. I read nothing on his face. And I wasn't going into the reason behind my question — not yet. A bit at a time until I got to the truth. I left Uncle Frank to his vegetables.

I sat in my car a while. I drummed on the wheel. I'd been hearing a great deal about my father. His life and personality, and more. Who killed him? Why? It was as if he died alone. He hadn't. Another person died with him — my mother. She was still a mystery to me, the unknown. I decided it was time to rectify that. And I knew only one person who could help me.

I crossed the Pennines for the second time.

10

A different Aunt Edna from a few days earlier; cooler, resigned.

'I knew you'd soon be back,' she said. She studied me as I took a seat. 'I was wrong, wasn't I? I have been doing some hard thinking, Jimmy. I have reached the conclusion that you have the right to know everything I can tell you.'

Haywire again. I had come here with the intention of browbeating Aunt Edna into talking. It was unnecessary. I recognised that she yearned to talk of the past. She perched on the edge of the sofa, hands clasped at her knees. I leaned back, and listened.

'Our father died when we were quite young. Mother died when Jenny was sixteen. I was already married to Alex. Sal was barely two and I was carrying Eric. Jenny came to live with us. We were always close, and grew closer.'

She smiled, happy to be releasing the

memories that had stayed bottled inside so long. She studied her hands, weighed her words. She spoke slowly, with long pauses.

'Jenny was the one with the looks, and I the one with the brains. I'm not claiming I was brilliant and she stupid, nothing like that. And certainly she was no dumb blonde. She was a little shy, and when you allied that to her looks it tended to make her appear somewhat haughty. She wasn't. There were boys around of course. But nothing very serious.

'Then there happened along Pete Ellis.' I noted the tinge of bitterness. 'He drove lorries at the time. He'd delivered a load in these parts and the weather had closed in so he was staying overnight. They met at the local dance hall. He was a charmer — but not a man I could take easily to. Too smooth, always there with a sharp retort, as if he had to prove he was better than you. I warned Jenny off him, and there occurred our only real bitter argument.

'She loved him! She was eighteen and

in love with the idea of being in love. He was just a year older. Then she discovered she was pregnant. I thought Pete would run and we'd never hear from him again. He didn't, and that is in his favour. You came along six months after the marriage. I never saw you. Two months earlier Alex and I had emigrated. A new job, a new chance. We couldn't put it off.'

She dabbed at her eyes, breathed deeply to control her emotions. I didn't move an inch, hardly seemed to breathe. I could think of nothing to say that might comfort her. It was her own battle.

'I never saw Jenny again,' she went on after a while. 'We wrote often. I was able to keep track of the deterioration in her marriage. I begged her to bring you and join us in Australia, and I think that was something she was pondering on. He often struck her, and you. He had a vicious temper with the drink inside him. There was some trouble with the police, though I don't know the details. But Jenny adored you. You were her life. You had your father's looks, but her gentleness of spirit.

'God! It tore me in half when I learned that she had died — and the way she died. Such bloody and mindless savagery. I had a bad time for a while. Nerves. I couldn't get her out of my mind. I saw her face everywhere. I wasn't giving much thought to you during this period. Only her. Then the months passed and I began to wonder. How had Jimmy taken this? I wrote to your grandmother. Her reply was terse and to the point. You were fine, and happy.

'I decided to find out for myself. I returned to England. Your grandmother insisted that you were a healthy and well adjusted boy. It was untrue. Ashen, nervous, almost mute. You were the unhappiest child imaginable.

'I was lost. I had no one to advise me. Alex was on the other side of the world. After two days I had packed my bags and was ready to leave. Then it struck me. I knew what Jenny would ask of me. I went to see your grandmother again. I asked if I could take you with me. Her response was grim. No, you would stay with her.

143

But I was determined now. Next day I went to the school. I waited until break. I shouted and you came to the railings. I asked if you wanted to come and live with me and my family and you nodded solemnly, put your hand in mine. It was all the answer I needed. We booked into a shabbey hotel in Manchester. Every moment I expected the police to knock on the door and arrest me for kidnapping. I needed papers for you. I got them.

'Everything went smoothly. You grew up fine, Jimmy. Within weeks you were a happy and normal youngster. I was proud of you. But you never mentioned Pete and Jenny, but for that one time on the plane. I told myself it was a blessing.'

We talked on. She talked about her own parents, her own childhood. Then I brought her back to more painful topics. I asked if she had kept the letters my mother wrote her. She shook her head.

'Go back to Australia, Jimmy,' she said. 'That is where you belong. Find Eric — go on a drunk. Find a regular girl. Stop meddling in this affair. There is

144

only pain and heart-ache for you here.'

In a way, she was right. But I had travelled too far down the road to give up now. If I did, I knew I would regret it, knew I would always wonder why my parents had to die. And it would be cowardice to turn back now. I had to live with myself.

Aunt Edna left the room for some moments, returned. Entwined around her fingers was a small and plain gold crucifix on a slender chain.

'I asked your grandmother for it and she gave it to me. My present to Jenny on her sixteenth birthday.'

She slipped the crucifix into my palm. I stared down at it. Vague memories began to stir, images I could never quite grasp, as if I was staring down a long tunnel into the past. The crucifix had a significance I couldn't comprehend. I thrust the ghosts to the back of my mind. I slipped the crucifix over my head. It was cool against my skin.

'And this,' she added.

A small coloured photograph. Two people, man and woman. He was dark, and the resemblance to myself startling. She was blonde and fair skinned, eyes clear blue. The hand that held the photograph began to shake a little.

'She was lovely,' I mumbled.

'The loveliest, Jimmy. And though you resemble that man — remember that inside you are her, that her heart beats inside you. It is important for you to remember that.'

And so it was. I had an evening out with her husband and stepson. We got drunk and I stayed the night. Mindless bliss encompassed me for a little while.

* * *

I rose early. My head still throbbed. I avoided the rush hour traffic and was soon back in Penningstone. I caught Dave Pearson on the building site where I first met him.

'Blackmail,' he said thoughtfully, pulling a wrinkled dog end from behind his ear and lighting it. 'You say Pete had something on Hanson, that Hanson

146

wasn't in on the brewery fiddle for the money?'

'So Hanson reckons. And I believe him.'

'It does have the hollow ring of truth. And Hanson was never the type who took risks — not when his precious integrity was involved — and especially not if it might cost him his beloved uniform,' he added drily. 'And it concerns a woman?'

I nodded, and once more recounted my latest confrontation with Hanson.

'A poser,' Dave mumbled absently. 'Hanson was never married, so the threat of information slipped to his wife is out. Now if the woman had a husband — that might be different. Pete could have put the screws on Hanson — threatened him with the husband. That has possibilities. But I don't like it.'

'Possibly he wanted to protect the woman?' I offered.

'Her honour — you mean?' Dave laughed loudly. 'I can't see that. Not Hanson.'

We swopped theories, got nowhere. Then Dave said, 'And Pete would need evidence. Word of mouth wouldn't be good enough from a man with Pete's reputation for stirring.'

'Photographs? Letters?'

'That's possible,' he mused.

'So where would he keep them — at the house?'

He glanced at me as if I was an idiot. 'The police would have sniffed them out. No. Not the house.'

'A safety deposit box?'

'Hardly Pete's style.' He laughed again. 'No, he'll have stashed them — if they ever existed — but God knows where.'

Dave hadn't been much help. But it was good to have someone to talk to.

I slowed down at the end of Livingstone Terrace. The key to number fifteen burned a hole in my pocket. But not yet. Too soon to face the horrors that house might possibly hold for me.

★ ★ ★

Sarah ambushed me in the passage as I arrived back at the Fox Inn. Her ability to appear from nowhere and be everywhere always confounded me. Now she struck her usual aggressive pose, and more; her lips stretched in a tight white line. Her voice was cool and cutting.

'Where have you been?'

Now it seemed I was to be treated like a naughty schoolboy. But I could see no reason not to answer, or lie. I told her I had stayed the night with a relative. And I pondered on her attitude, her coldness. She soon put me in the picture.

'The bolts on the front door,' she explained sharply. 'I like to feel safe in my bed. In future, have the courtesy to inform me when you intend to stay out all night. The key is a privilege, not a right.'

Duly rebuked, the lesson over, and she seemed to soften visibly. And I knew she didn't give a damn if the door was bolted or not. She was simply getting something out of her system, though what — I wouldn't have liked to hazard a guess.

Suddenly, her hand shot out and clipped my chin, and her peculiar scent was getting to me even in the draughty coolness of this passage.

'George is going into Penningstone later — the bank, and other business. I'll come to your room, and teach you not to cheat on me.'

She had given me the answer. Still riled because I had slept with another woman. Jealousy? No, too shallow for Sarah. She was insulted because I hadn't found her enough of a woman.

My arm circled her waist. I didn't give a damn if George was lurking about someplace. Then I suddenly swallowed the urge to scream as her foot scraped the length of my shin. She stepped back quickly, smiled slyly, then she was gone. I stared at the door she had passed through. Then I shook my head. She was an enigma I couldn't figure.

I sat at the table by the window. Outside, the air was clear. The wind whipped across the open terrain. As always, the hills constantly changed colour. There was a raw and staggering beauty out there, but I couldn't ponder on that now. I put all such thoughts from my mind, and concentrated.

A blank sheet of paper before me, a

pen. But where to start? The obvious. The beginning — the nightmare, awakening in my bed on the other side of the world. I wrote in the form of a diary. Day one. I listed the people I had spoken to. I recorded our conversations as fully as I could remember; in some instances, almost word for word. My thoughts at the time. The conclusions I later reached.

The blister on my palm had healed, caused no discomfort. I wrote steadily until my fingers cramped. I flexed them, picked up the pen and wrote some more. The words began to flow more easily. I heard a car pulling away. I wondered if it was George on his way to the bank, if Sarah had meant what she said. Would she come? I didn't dwell on it. I wrote on. Ideas spun around my mind; theories and complications. And I discovered I was haunted by a man I had met when I was little more than a child. What would Charlie Grey have done? Or, what did Charlie do? Nag, nag, nag; that had been his formula; nag at the mind until something snapped.

The feet on the landing and the door

opening came almost simultaneously. I spun around. Sarah leaned her back to the wall. She smiled invitingly. Then a shadow crossed her face. She stepped forward with a purpose.

'Why are you acting so guilty?' The cold tones of the schoolmistress had returned. 'Show me.'

I stood quickly, blocked her path as she tried to dodge past. Her hand went for the sheets of paper and my palm slapped down before she could snatch them.

'Personal?' I snapped.

'Oh?' The smile was back, teasing. 'Secrets from Sarah? And aren't we touchy?' Her hand cupped my chin. 'Is this the story that will make you rich and famous? Is this the story of how you solved a seventeen year old mystery?'

She was taunting, getting under my skin. Her hips pressed on mine, rotated. I was sinking. I needed her so bad it hurt. Her hand wound into my hair, tugged my head back. The need to lose myself inside her was unbearable.

* * *

She slipped from my side and dressed quickly, tossed her hair free from her dress. I lay back. I lit a cigarette from the pack on the bedside table. I watched her move casually to the window. The room lay still, no sound louder than the double heartbeat of the two people it held. I broke the silence. My voice was low yet it seemed to fill the room.

'Do you love George, Sarah?'

She turned slowly. For a second time I noted the serenity on her face. Despite her moods, I decided Sarah was a woman at peace with herself.

'George is George. I don't know what I would do without him,' she said vaguely.

'Is that love? Needing someone?'

I had no answer. I had loved in my own shallow way, but never been in love. Until the last week or so I doubted if there had ever been any real depth to my emotions. But I was learning, growing up fast.

'I don't remember a time when he wasn't there,' she continued, then a small smile played at the corners of her mouth. 'Comfortable, that's what I am.'

'Does he know we have slept together — made love?'

'Slept together. How quaint.' Her smile broadened. 'We have never slept together, have we? Or made love? There is only one word to describe what we do in that bed, and I won't use it. I think it is a fact that we barely like each other — you and I. We fulfil a need that is missing. My excuse is loneliness, a fear that the world has passed me by.' She sighed. 'And of course George doesn't know. You are testimony to that. He'd hurt you, sweetheart — if he ever found out.'

That sent a chill along my spine. I changed the subject. I asked how well she had known my father.

'Not well.' She leaned back against the window sill. 'If you are asking what I think you are — the answer is no. I was very young then.'

I let that pass. I recalled Larry Jenkin's description of her. I asked what attracted my father to the Fox Inn. I knew he was unpopular, so why did he constantly return.

'Maybe he was a masochist.' There was a lightness in her tone, though I wondered if she might be close to the truth. 'Pete was quite a man. You are very like him, yet you lack his attractiveness. You seem a boy by comparison. He even got along with my mum, which was quite a feat. She lived in this room.' Her eyes flicked around without sentimental interest. 'He spent quite a bit of time chatting to her.'

That seemed out of character, yet somehow it didn't surprise me. Nothing I learned about my father surprised me. I asked how well she knew Vic Hanson.

'Old groper.' She laughed. 'I have always known him — but how well — who can say? I see him here. We exchange banter. But I can't say we have ever held an intimate fireside chat. No, I wouldn't say I know him well, only superficially. He hated Pete — I do know that. Every time Pete spoke to him he winced. But don't ask me why.'

'Was George scared of my father?'

'George wasn't, and isn't, scared of

anybody. George is an independent man. And George is a good man. He tolerated my mother all those years. He felt it was his duty.' Her eyes held mine. 'And don't push George too far, sweetheart. This sarcastic 'sport' business has begun to get on his nerves.'

'But it was George in my room the other night?'

Her eyes blazed a second, cooled quicker. 'No. And I don't believe anybody was in your room. You were drunk. You could hardly stand up.'

I couldn't figure out if her denial was the truth. And I didn't bother to point out that I was groggy because I had been punched in the stomach. It was pointless. She would believe what she wanted to believe. She began to tap on the sheets of paper that still lay on the table with a painted fingernail.

'What would happen if I picked these up and read them?' she asked.

'I'd break your wrist,' I replied without emotion.

She glanced at me, lips spreading. It was a genuine smile she bestowed on me. A touch of sunlight. I suddenly understood that Sarah was my friend.

'I don't think you'd do that,' she said softly. 'I don't think you have the right mentality to hit a woman. I think that underneath your swagger you are as soft as putty. Not that I think you are a coward — you are obviously not that.' She shrugged. 'Anyway, I don't want to see what you've written. I don't think I care to know what you think of me, or George, or the village. You are a stranger. You might see what we don't. You might come close to the truth. And the truth can hurt.'

There was the sound of a car pulling onto the car-park. She sighed, moved to the door.

'The master has returned to his castle.' She turned, her voice suddenly sober. 'That was the last time, sweetheart. Bloody stupid of me to start it. I'm content with George.'

The door closed quietly behind her, and the world was darker, lonelier.

11

Early evening. I had completed my notes and locked them away in my suitcase. Then I changed my mind. It seemed people entered this room at the slightest whim. I retrieved and pushed them into my pocket.

I went downstairs, outside, and into my car. Ten minutes later I was back. Few customers in the bars. Sarah and Lesley chatted idly. I drifted around in search of George. I heard a noise in the cellar, the scrape of wood on stone. I pushed open the door and soundlessly entered.

I was in a dungeon-like room. Damp walls and the air icy cold. A single naked light bulb dangled on a cord from a low ceiling. It cast shadows around the place. I conjured images of emaciated prisoners chained to the walls, screaming under the lash of the torturer's whip. A single shadow moved against the far wall, loomed long, then shallow.

I squatted on my heels at the top of the stairs. I watched him work for a while. His back was to me, then he half turned. He wiped a film of sweat from his face, coughed into the back of his hand.

I lit a cigarette and he spun at the sudden noise and flare of the match. I recognised rage on his face, hatred. It chilled my blood. He took one quick stride towards me, then stilled.

'What the bloody hell are you doing down here?' he snarled. 'Creeping about the place like a bloody sewer rat.'

Why did this man hate me? Over and over I had asked myself this question. Dislike, possibly. That was an easy emotion to understand. It was possible to dislike someone for no saner motive than the colour of their socks. But hate was different. Hate came from all the senses; mind and heart and soul. And he had hated me right from the first moment he saw me.

'The door was half open, sport,' I said flatly. 'I heard a noise and came to investigate like a good citizen. And seeing as how you brought it up — creeping. Why were you in my room the other night?'

'Still nagging about that! You're worse than a bloody old woman.' He almost spat in my direction. 'I already told you, squire. Nobody was in your room. Maybe you have a persecution complex.'

'Could be, sport. And everybody keeps telling me there was nobody in my room. But somehow I get the feeling they realise they are spouting a load of crap. And it had to be you, sport. Wouldn't like to roll up your trouser legs and prove me wrong? The bruise should still be showing.'

'Go play with yourself!' His belly laugh filled the cellar, echoed around eerily. He went back to stacking his crates. 'You're a worm, squire. You slide across the earth on your belly. You can chop bits off a worm and it grows back to normal. Insensitive creatures are worms. Can't take a hint. Keep coming back to have another bit chopped off. Best idea is to stamp on them, grind them into the dirt.'

'That sounds like a threat, sport.'

Again he turned. I sensed danger in

his stance, and more, the chill wind of death. I shivered and the cigarette shook in my hand. He noticed. His smile was that of the serpent.

'You're nervous, squire,' he said. 'And I don't issue threats. I'm a doer, not a talker.'

I reckoned he wasn't joking, or bluffing. The shaking had ceased. I took a long drag on the cigarette.

'Where were you on the night of the murders, sport?' I asked in a flat monotone.

The question clearly amused him. 'Right here, squire. Where I am every night.'

'And you didn't step out for a while?'

His amusement deepened. He chuckled in his throat. 'No, squire — I didn't. Is that what you newshounds call the third degree?'

'I think that's the Gestapo, sport, or the FBI.' I tossed the cigarette away and it landed at his feet. Smoke spiralled upwards. 'What about the Sunday night before the murders? My dad was here, wasn't he?'

'So?'

I didn't blink as I fixed my eyes on his. 'I just wondered if anything unusual happened that night.'

'Not that I recollect,' he answered, and I read nothing on his face. 'You hinting at something, squire?'

'No.' I shrugged. 'Though something puzzles me, sport — why haven't you told me to pack my bags and shove off?'

'I run a business, squire. Why ask?'

'Just wondered,' I said lightly. 'What with me getting attacked by phantoms and disturbing your sleep.'

I pushed to my feet. He remained in the centre of the room, motionless, watching me under those bushy eyebrows. He hardly seemed to breathe. Again he reminded me of the serpent, waiting to strike, tear the flesh of a mouse. And I knew that was how he saw me. A mouse, an inconsequential mouse. My temper suddenly hit the surface.

'You're a cold-blooded bastard, sport, and gutless. It takes a peculiar sort of animal to blow a man to bits — and a woman. That's really special. She was just twenty-six, sport. What did she do that she deserved to die?'

No reaction. Nothing. His skin glistened under the harsh light, eyes as cold as marble.

'One of you brave bastards butchered her, sport.' I was aware that my voice was rising, tried to control it. 'I don't know which one — but I'll find out. And if it was you — I'll have you, sport!'

Still he hadn't moved. I spun on my heels. I now knew I had it in me to kill a man, blast his life to shreds.

★ ★ ★

I was in the saloon bar, locked in conversation with Lesley's 'maybe' boy-friend. The subject was Test cricket; something with a wider appeal than sheep. Others joined in, found ourselves involved in a quiz. I kept half an eye on my watch. I counted off the seconds until it reached eight o'clock. I pushed back my chair and sauntered to the bar. I hovered there, then slipped through the door. Another door and I was in

163

the passage. I had reached the toilets. A man stepped out. We nodded. I had never seen him before. I counted to three, then moved quickly. I unlatched the back door and glanced over my shoulder. The length of the passage stood empty. I slipped outside.

I allowed my eyes to adjust to the darkness. A deep pool of light flooded through the frosted window of the taproom. I ducked under the sill, crept past. I was at the side of the pub. I broke into a trot. I leapt over the stone wall. I cursed as my foot sank into something moist. I walked steadily. Down the sharp incline, jumped the stream yet contrived to get my feet wet. I climbed the other side and crossed a field.

My car was on the track where I had left it earlier, tucked out of sight of the road in a hollow. I was inside, feet slippery on the pedals. The engine fired first time. No headlights until I reached the road, which I met only thirty yards past the bridge. No traffic. I didn't push it. I drove at a steady thirty. I was soon on the outskirts of Penningstone and parking my car at the end of Livingstone Terrace.

I left the comfort of the interior, kept the door open. I strode quickly along the back of the terrace. I counted off the houses. I reached number fifteen. I paused. The house loomed before me; the dusty and dark windows beckoning. My heart began to thump in my chest. I unlatched the gate and stepped into the tiny yard.

I went through the motions of knocking, likened myself to a ghoul. I imagined the door opening, a man standing there, a man who looked exactly like me. We argued. I opened my coat, pointed the gun at his chest. I pulled the trigger. One, two, three. With my eyes closed I pulled the trigger again. I raced back the way I came. I reached the car, tossed the imaginary gun into the back and flung myself inside. I hit the ignition and slammed the door in a single movement. The wheels spun, caught hold. My pulse rate slowed. I put the needle back to thirty again. I was soon back in Saddlebridge, reversing my footsteps.

I inched open the back door. Nobody in the passage. I was inside. I glanced down. My shoes were a mess but I doubted if anybody would notice. My breathing was almost normal. I strolled to the saloon bar and slid back into my seat. The quiz was still in progress. I picked up the thread and joined in. Nobody seemed to notice I'd been away. The time on my watch read eight twenty-three.

Twenty-three minutes!

Nothing! No time at all. And the murderer could have carried out the operation much quicker.

What if he had left the car at the side of the pub? Possibly he had. He'd be taking a chance of being spotted coming or going, but so had I by leaving my car on the dirt track. Though, I surmised, in the middle of Winter when the murders took place, that was the more feasible possibility. I'd checked. The dirt track was little more than a short cut, not leading directly to a farm, and not likely to be used on a wintery night. And again, most of the people I was interested in wouldn't drive to the Fox Inn. They lived locally. They walked. It would have aroused suspicion if the murderer had driven to the pub on that one particular night. Anyway, I had proved to my own satisfaction that to use the Fox Inn as an alibi was no alibi at all. And seventeen years earlier, Charlie Grey had undoubtedly reached the same conclusion.

★ ★ ★

An hour later I entered the taproom for the first time in several days. There were five or six customers, Hanson and Kent amongst them, but no Uncle Frank.

I still wasn't popular. Eyes flicked in my direction then slid away. I was what is known as a bad smell under the nose. I found it didn't disturb me. My favourite chair was empty, and after collecting a pint from a scowling George I sat down. I waited patiently, took the odd sip of beer, smoked. George glanced at his watch and moved to shout 'time' in the other bars. I took the opportunity to wander over to Vic Hanson who now stood alone.

167

'I'd like a word, Vic,' I whispered in his ear.

'Bugger off!'

Short and sweet and to the point. He tried to turn away but I wasn't having that. I twisted him around.

'How'd it be if I announced you as a thief, Vic?'

I grinned, watched him waver. My father had blackmailed him, now I was doing the same. It gave me a strange and grim satisfaction. I nodded to my lonely corner, and after a few seconds to consider, he followed me there. I was aware of Sammy Kent watching us. His eyes bored holes into my skull.

Hanson sat uncomfortably, twisted, avoided the curious eyes that turned our way. George was back, took us in with a quick glance but showed nothing.

'What the hell do you want?' Hanson hissed.

'The truth,' I replied softly, coldly. 'Where were you on the night of the murders?'

'I don't need to answer you!' He shook his head, then he shrugged. 'Here of

168

course. No secret. I never left the place. Arrived at seven and didn't leave until midnight.'

'And plenty of witnesses who will swear to that,' I commented drily.

'Enough.' He sniggered. 'I say again — I don't know who killed Pete Ellis — and I don't care. To me he was an anonymous hero.'

A knot of temper tightened my stomach. I pointed out that this hero had blasted the life out of a young woman that night. He wriggled, mumbled something I couldn't pick out. I decided it was time to play my ace.

'What about the previous Sunday — were you here?'

'It's likely.' His answer came slow and furtive.

'I'd guarantee that you were, Vic. My dad was here; tell me about the fight.' He shook his head, claimed not to understand. 'I think you do, Vic. You must have heard what brought me here. The reporter who contacted me. Your version differs from hers. You told her there was a fight in here that Sunday night — that my dad was involved.'

'She misheard,' he mumbled. 'Or she made it up.'

'No, she didn't make it up.' I leaned closer, and the lie came easy to my tongue. 'I've spoken to her. She remembers distinctly. You told her about a fight in this very room. Later you denied it. But I still think that fight took place.'

'Okay!' he snapped. 'I told her. But there was still no fight. I'd have told her anything to keep her interested. She kept licking her lips and pouting, leading me on.'

'It seems women are always leading you on, Vic. It must be your dynamic personality.' The sarcasm dripped from my tongue. 'And let's have the truth. Put me wise about the fight.'

'No fight!' He was standing. I gripped his elbow and he knocked my hand away. 'Enough! You can stand on the bar if you like and tell the bloody world why I lost my job at the brewery. I don't care! I'll not have that threat hanging over me! Not from a bastard like you! I've been through it all before.'

His voice had risen. Faces turned in our direction. Hanson strode to the bar and the comfort of his mates. I heard his nervous laughter, his touch of bravado. I leaned back and slowly finished my beer. Only George and a few friends now; Hanson and Kent, another man I couldn't put a name to; single and lonely men with no wives to check their movements. Their eyes followed me as I left. The release of tension was almost audible.

I heard the click of ash trays in the saloon bar. I presumed Sarah was clearing up. I climbed the stairs slowly.

I cautiously opened the door to my room. I snapped on the light and stood on the threshhold. I half hoped somebody might be there. I was in the mood to punch and claw.

The stench hit me a physical blow!

I recoiled. I clamped a hand over my mouth and nose. It lay against the whiteness of the pillow — the decomposing body of a black cat. The air seemed to be alive around it, a storm

171

of scavenging fleas. I spun out of the room, slammed the door behind me, into the bathroom. Just in time. My guts exploded through my mouth, pain racked my ribs, sweat poured from me. I recovered slowly. I washed my face, swallowed a glass of cold water.

I waited on the landing. Her footsteps warned me. She saw me as soon as she rounded the bend. She paused. Her head cocked to one side in question. She came closer.

'Oh, God,' she whispered. 'What has happened now?'

I nodded towards my room. She hesitated, then swung open the door gingerly, took no more than a single step inside. I asked if I was drunk now, if my imagination was playing tricks. Her face was ashen, teeth clenched, but there was sympathy in her eyes when she looked at me.

'Tomorrow,' she said quietly, 'you leave.'

I didn't understand. 'Why?'

'Isn't that obvious?' I didn't respond. 'This whole business is getting out of

control. Too many games — if it was ever a game. Someone is going to get hurt — and that someone is likely to be you.'
Stupidly, I asked if she cared. 'I care enough not to want to see you hurt.'

'And the other night,' I said. 'Do you still say you heard no one on the stairs?'

'I do,' she insisted, then paused. 'But perhaps there was someone in your room. I just don't know.'

And I think I finally believed that she was giving me the truth. 'Who is doing this, Sarah? And why?'

'I don't know who — the why is obvious. They want you out of this village. They remember your father, how it was after his death.'

'Who killed my parents, Sarah?'

'I don't know.' She met my eyes. I knew she wasn't lying. 'And I don't think anyone will ever discover his identity.'
She was wrong on that point. 'I'll make out your bill in the morning.'

I shook my head. I wasn't going anywhere. She studied me, then shrugged wearily. She pointed to the room opposite.

She told me to sleep there tonight. She'd see to my own room in the morning.

I didn't argue. I was shattered, but slept fitfully.

12

'Why do you torment me, Jimmy?'

Oh, hell!

It was like butting my head against a brick wall. The self-pitying whine in his voice infuriated me. Grandmother was serving a customer in the post office, Uncle Frank sat opposite me at the kitchen table. We sipped tea from ancient mugs. He had yet to meet my eyes.

And why hadn't Uncle Frank returned to the Fox Inn since the night he came to my room? Since my arrival in Saddlebridge, that was the only occasion he'd been there. And why that night? Why the whisky bottle to loosen his tongue?

'You were in the Fox Inn on the night of the murders?' I asked for the second time.

'I told you — yes.' He gripped the mug so tightly I wondered if it would explode in his hand. 'I was there. All night.'

'In the taproom?'

'Always the taproom,' he mumbled. 'It was packed that night — I remember. A football match on the television. There was no TV in the saloon bar in those days. So George brought his own into the taproom so we could watch. They crowded in from the other bars.'

Very interesting. The television, a crowded bar. 'Did you notice anybody slip out?'

His gaze concentrated on the table. 'Such as who?'

'Vic Hanson,' I prodded. 'George Slater. Sammy Kent.'

'No.' His voice had risen. 'Nobody left! I've been through this before — we all have. That fat policeman. He asked the same questions. He kept coming here. Whenever I showed my face on the street he'd pop from nowhere. Blowing smoke in my face, asking the same questions until I grew dizzy. They took him off the case, but still he pestered us.'

'He wanted to find the killer, Frank — don't you?'

'No!' His fist thumped the table. The

mugs rattled. 'I only want to be left in peace.'

'So do I. But I won't find peace until I get the bastard who killed them. You can inform your pals of that. I'm not quitting on this.'

He muttered something about understanding how I felt. But Uncle Frank understood nothing. He surely didn't understand me. His tongue began to work again.

'I didn't do it, Jimmy. Nor any of the others. We couldn't. We were at the pub.'

It was no answer. I'd checked. Frank, Slater, Hanson, and Kent; all had vehicles at the time of the murders. I knew Frank had a shotgun, and asked him about it.

'The police took it away,' he said. 'To check. They gave it me back.'

'I doubt if that would prove anything more than whether it had been fired recently,' I said. 'And you used it a lot, Frank. I remember that.'

'Only rabbits and birds and stuff, nothing more than that.'

It was much the same as with the rest

of them in these parts. I pointed out that they were a right bunch of big-game hunters in Saddlebridge.

'But we are not killers,' he re-affirmed. 'If I'd known who killed Pete I'd have told the police — believe me.'

I didn't. There was a bitter taste of contempt in my mouth for Uncle Frank. I asked if he had been in the taproom on the Sunday before the murders. I received the same reaction as from Hanson — furtive. He claimed he didn't understand.

'I'll explain,' I said coldly. 'My father was in the taproom of the Fox Inn that night. It was late, after closing time. Just George and a few cronies. There was an argument, a fight. My dad was involved. I'd like to know who he had the fight with — and who was there.'

Frank went through the pantomime of scratching his head. He was one hell of a ham actor. And still his eyes refused to meet mine!

'Yes. Pete was there,' he said vaguely, with an expression to match. 'But I don't recall who else.'

'I'll help,' I said testily. 'Start with George Slater, and the other regulars — the local lads who are invited to stay on for a sociable drink and chat — how about Sammy Kent and Vic Hanson?'

'Maybe.' He shook his head. 'I don't remember. But there couldn't have been a fight, Jimmy. I'd have remembered that.'

Yes, he would! And it was hopeless. I wanted to take him by the throat and shake him. I told him to ponder on it, that I'd be back — and I would. Hell, I would!

★ ★ ★

Jesus!

I never had to go looking for Sammy Kent. He always contrived to find me.

I hesitated with my hand on the door. I shrugged, decided what the hell, and slipped behind the wheel.

He lay sprawled in the passenger seat. He'd been there for some time. The air was sour with tobacco smoke. Wearily, I asked how he'd got inside and he rattled a bunch of keys in his pocket.

'These kiddie cars are as easy to open as a tin of sardines,' he said smugly. 'A twist and a tug and in you go.'

'It's illegal, Sammy,' I pointed out.

'That's okay. I know you won't report me, sunshine.' He lolled back, his right arm hanging loose behind the seat. It made me nervous. 'Let's go for a drive in your fancy motor.'

I shook my head, summoned a grin, sniggered something about his sexual preferences. His skin coloured to that ripe purple again. I wondered if I might induce a heart attack if I pushed a little harder. I decided against. I didn't want his grisly carcass on my hands.

'One day you are going to choke on that fat lip,' he threatened; cooled, tried his smug grin. 'I hear you've been taking dead cats to bed. That's kinky, sunshine.'

'Guess so, Sammy,' I said evenly. 'Could be the animal smell reminded me of someone.'

I suddenly knew the identity of the man who attacked me in my room. But it couldn't be! I shook the idea from my mind. Kent was asking if I was a junky, if I stuck needles in my arm and popped pills. He reckoned I might be a hippie.

'Hippies are drop-outs who play at being scruffy,' I pointed out. 'With me it comes natural. Anyway, hippies are as out of date as you, Sammy. Bloody dinosaurs.'

'That lip again.' He leaned closer, and I felt a shimmer of apprehension run down my spine. I wished I knew what the hell he was doing with that right hand. 'And I think you are a junky. I don't think you know what day of the week it is. Why else would you take a dead cat to bed with you, accuse folk of prowling about your room in the dark?'

He paused, considering his words, and I realised he was finally getting to the point.

'And the latest — a mythical fight in the taproom. Saying your old man was involved in an argument, a fight. Drugs, that's the answer. You're hallucinating, sunshine.'

'I don't think so, Sammy. And who

came hotfoot to you with this snippet of information? Hanson? Frank?'

My smile was for real as I twisted to face him. He really was a moronic piece of filth. I hadn't finished.

'If the fight hadn't taken place, Sammy, you wouldn't be here. You're scared shitless. And that makes me wonder. Could have been you who killed them. Out of the back door of the pub. Drive to Penningstone. Bang, bang. And was it you who had the fight with my father that Sunday night?'

His howl of derision stunned me. His head rocked back.

'That's funny, sunshine,' he said. 'If Pete Ellis had picked a fight with me — he wouldn't have been around to get himself murdered. He'd already have been in hospital with both legs in traction.'

He'd scored a good point there. I asked a question that sobered him instantly, as it was meant to. I asked why he hated my father.

'You've been informed, sunshine.' His voice was icy cold. 'He let my son drown.' I pointed out that my father

182

couldn't swim. He took a deep breath. 'An excuse! I went back to the reservoir days later. It was pointed out to me exactly where my son drowned. I waded out. No more than five feet of water! Pete Ellis hadn't the guts to wade out until water reached his neck. So yellow it cost my son his life!'

He almost jumped from the car. The door slammed. I watched him until he disappeared. I wondered if he was right. Had his son drowned in five feet of water? I doubted if I'd ever know the truth.

I'd given enough thought to Sammy Kent for now. There was something I had to do, a task I could put off no longer. I plunged the car into gear before I changed my mind.

* * *

I pushed the key into the lock of number fifteen, Livingstone Terrace. I hesitated, then twisted. The door opened noiselessly.

Dust rose in the air to greet me.

The light was dim through the murky windows. I guessed this was almost exactly how it had been on the night of the murders. The police had searched the house but taken nothing. And grandmother had touched nothing. So the room lay frozen in time, encapsuled. There were ashes in the grate from a long dead fire.

A weariness flooded over me, a deep sadness. A voice at the back of my mind told me to leave, that there was nothing here for me, only pain. I ignored that voice. My eyes traversed about me.

The room was surprisingly small; impossible to take more than a stride in any direction without colliding with some article of furniture, the ceiling so low I could have reached up to clear the cobwebs. In one corner I pulled aside a curtain to reveal a staircase. Beneath the dust the carpet was barely worn. The hairs on my neck bristled as I climbed the stairs. I was walking backwards into the past, into the darkest recesses of memory. The boards creaked eerily.

Christ! I was suddenly terrified. I wiped

my sweating palms. I took slow breaths to control myself. I paused on the landing. A brief hesitation and I pushed open the door on my right.

A scene from an old black and white movie; a scene in which time stood still. The double bed had the sheets pulled back as if waiting for someone to slip between them. From the dressing table my parents smiled at me from a silvered frame; a jar of cream, a small bottle of perfume, a hairbrush, other odds and ends scattered about the surface.

I opened drawers: filled with neatly folded shirts and blouses, pullovers, ties and socks. I glanced into the wardrobe. Suits and jackets hung neatly on their hangers on one side, dresses and skirts on the other.

I left that room and crossed the landing to the smaller room at the back. A single bed, a set of drawers, peeling posters on the wall. Footballers dressed in red and white, grinning out from the mists of time. No clothes. I presumed these had followed me to the post office.

I moved to the window. In the distance

it was possible to make out the hills through the mist. I recognised the Peak, the narrow road that would eventually snake its way to Saddlebridge.

Down the stairs again, into the cramped back room. A sofa, chairs, more ashes in the grate, a small television in the corner. This was a scene from the nightmare, the beginnings of terror that came with a knock on the door.

I took a deep breath, then passed through the door into the tiny kitchen.

Almost unconsciously, I forced myself to re-enact the nightmare. I fell to my knees. The gold crucifix hung from my neck, caught in shafts of strange light. I touched it, withdrew my hand as it burned. A blackness stole over me. I was entering a tunnel, running to reach a pinprick of light at the other end. I was then holding someone in my arms. Her skin was pale and hair a dull yellow. I shook her, pleaded. She didn't respond. Her blue eyes were open and stared into mine. I grew frightened. I called her name. Again, and again, I called. Then my mouth opened. A terrible scream filled the room, beat around me, tore at me.

Something shattered in my brain. I choked on bile and pain. I spun, lurched to my feet. My eyes rolled in their sockets, took in the ceiling and walls, the window. I noticed the dark streak near the foot of the door. I saw a small boy, dressed in white shirt and blue jeans. The sun was hot through the window. His face was flushed. He held a football, reached for the door handle. The ball fell. He made a pretence at kicking it. His foot scuffed along the door. The door was freshly painted and he examined the mark he had made. His heart tightened. He rubbed at the mark, knew he was making it worse. He knew his father would belt him when he saw it.

They flooded back — the long-forgotten memories. The man and woman I shared this house with those long years ago. I now knew that I had loved them both. The man because he was big and strong and generous, and my father. I feared him though. I feared the sting of his open palm. I feared his treatment of my mother. I loved her also. There was a gentleness about her. I often caught her glancing at me, noted the pain that registered in her eyes. I knew she was unhappy. I knew how much I meant to her, and that frightened me. I was too young to carry such burdens.

I wiped a hand across my forehead, surprised to find a wetness there. My legs were stiff as I moved. I glanced into the back room, at the television in the corner. It seemed absurdly small and antique. I cast my mind back to that night. I could almost see the footballers flickering across the screen. I smiled. I wondered who had won the match. The idea struck me as strange, that I should ponder on something so irrelevant.

Into the front room I moved. I began to finger the crucifix, turned it over. I could see her again. She smiled. The crucifix shone brightly against the darkness of her sweater, catching the light and reflecting it. I could smell her perfume clearly. She constantly swept the long yellow hair from her face. I controlled the urge to speak to her. She was long dead, seventeen years dead. But I was happy to have seen her, for now I had a memory, and for me she would live on, never forgotten. It gave me a warmth, an understanding of myself, and as Aunt Edna had told me — her heart beat in my chest.

And I understood much more. I understood an old woman who came to this house. I understood why she came. Perhaps there was a form of life after death; but in the same instant I knew that that life only existed in the minds of those who wanted to believe.

I stepped onto the street. Everything was familiar to me now. My mind and memory were clear. I remembered my childhood as no one had ever remembered before. I recognised the individual cracks in the pavement, the stones of the houses, the corners and alleyways, the earth, the very sky above my head. My feet had trod these paths many times. I walked on, then walked some more.

It was an old school from Victorian days. Children played in the schoolyard, kicked footballs much the same as I had done, the girls a separate clique near the railings. In one of the rooms my name had been carved on a desk. I wondered if it remained. I decided I didn't care. I remembered, and that was enough.

I crossed the road to the phone box. He hadn't rung me, so I decided to ring him. A few quick words. Sure, he had meant to get in touch but had been too busy. Sure. Okay. Tonight. He gave me a time and a place.

13

The stripper turned her back, skin as pink as a salmon in the spotlight. She glanced over her shoulder. Her smile clicked on and off dramatically. The G-string fell away in her hand, circled over her head. She spun to face the audience, winked, then disappeared through the curtains.

The room filled with applause and whistling, then settled, replaced by the chatter of voices and the ring of beer glasses.

I sat on a stool by the bar, Sergeant Cooper beside me. His eyes constantly swept the room. It was filled with male bodies. No seats remained untaken. Men leaned on the walls at the back. Sergeant Cooper glanced my way and nudged me in the ribs.

'Stag night at the Star. The only night in the week when Penningstone approaches sin.' He wiped the beer froth from his lips. 'And this is the best place and best night for picking up information. You wouldn't guess it — but half the CID in Penningstone is scattered about this room. Sex and beer. A heady mix, loosens tongues and minds. Gossip mostly, who's flush and who's broke, but when you tot it up it usually comes to something.

'They know who I am, but that doesn't count for a toss. They read cheap magazines and watch the telly. So they think all coppers are either bent or thick. So they set out to prove they are brighter than you. But they forget the beer in their gut. They've had tits waggled before their eyes all night and they're mesmerised. They think of the old woman sat at home. Not always a pleasant thought. So they decide to compensate by making a clown out of a thick-headed copper.'

Though interested, I wasn't here for his particular philosophy on life. I asked if he had gone through the seventeen year old reports. He nodded glumly.

'Brought back memories, some pleasant,

some not so pleasant. There was little that might help you.'

I mentioned a few names. Frank Ellis, Vic Hanson, Sammy Kent, George Slater. Then another name entered my mind, a name I had been giving a great deal of thought to lately — Robbie Sandford. His memory was good.

'Nothing interesting on Slater, Hanson, or Sandford. No reason why they should want to kill Pete. Now Kent made some threats a few years earlier — concerned the drowning of his son.'

We went deeper into the death of Sammy Kent's son, why Kent had blamed my father. I mentioned that Kent claimed his son died in five feet of water.

'I never heard that said,' Cooper admitted. 'Though possible, it sounds unlikely. The reservoir is deep. A depth of five feet would place the boy close to the bank. And anyway, the weather is a major factor. In a dry spell the level can drop several feet a day. There'd be no way to point out exactly where the boy drowned.'

I experienced a flood of relief. I didn't

want to believe my father had watched a young boy drown and not tried to save him.

'And your Uncle Frank,' he said. 'Did you know he served time?'

I coughed, spat beer onto the bar. No, I bloody well didn't!

'A long time ago,' he said, ignoring my outburst. 'Just after he completed his National Service. He stayed in the south, worked in a market garden. He attacked a woman. A sexual assault. Minor by present day standards. No violence, no penetration. Collected him three years though. He served two. He returned to Saddlebridge and has had no involvement with the police since.'

'Was this widely known in Saddlebridge?'

'Unlikely. We didn't spread it around. It happened on the south coast. Not a mind-boggling case, not gruesome enough to make the Sunday papers, out of reach of the locals. I don't think he would have much of a problem keeping it quiet.'

Christ! The things you learned about

194

people. Uncle Frank an old lag!

The lights dimmed. The pink spotlight hit the stage. She was around forty, and carried little spare meat. She wasn't what the lads had come to see. She peeled quickly to shorten the agony. Only a spattering of applause greeted the end of her routine. I resumed my conversation with Sergeant Cooper.

'Yes,' he mused. 'Alibis are a bitch at the best of times. This case was no exception. Not that we had a prime suspect; we didn't, other than what was festering in old Charlie's brain. And you are right, half the male population of the village were in the Fox Inn that night. And if anybody stepped out during the relevant period, nobody noticed, or if they did, they were not saying.'

I'd drunk too much, and in the company of a dedicated policeman. No way was he allowing me to drive back to Saddlebridge. I spent the night on the sofa in his living room.

* * *

The sun shone from a cloudless sky, the fresh breeze of morning felt good in my lungs and on my face. I had learned that in this part of the world no two days dawned alike; the sun and rain alternated.

A small church, hardly larger than the Fox Inn. I strolled the graveyard at the back. Some of the dates on the headstones went back over a hundred years, to a time I found impossible to imagine.

It didn't take long to find the grave I sought. A simple headstone, names and dates carved neatly into it. I found it meant little to me. There were no tears in my eyes. They were nothing now. Dust under the soil. Not human; no hearts or brains, no blood to nourish them. And I had no flowers. I needed no flowers to remember. I stood there for some time, locked in my own thoughts. I thought of her, my mother. I wondered what would have become of her if she'd lived — and me. I decided it was pointless to dwell on something so abstract. I moved to the wooden bench in the corner. I lit a cigarette, leaned back, closed my eyes. The cigarette burned through and scorched my fingers. I let it fall. I allowed my mind to drift backwards.

The grey light of the post office. I gazed up at the faces that surrounded me. I wondered why these faces were so white, clothes so drab. Grandmother caught hold of me. She pushed a comb through my hair. I wanted to tell her I hated her, but lacked the courage.

We were outside. People watched us dolefully. Cameras clicked. We were in a big car. It moved slowly. We didn't travel far, a short journey up the hill to the church. More people watching. More cameras clicked.

Inside, I sat at the front between grandmother and Uncle Frank. Their faces were devoid of emotion, though I noted the redness around grandmother's eyes. The coffins lay in front of us. A man was speaking. He was round and tubby, almost bald. He had a cold. He often dabbed at his nose with a handkerchief.

He praised the departed souls. I knew

197

he meant my parents, because I had been told that was why we were here — to bury them. It was all right if I cried, but I wasn't allowed to fidget. I was to show respect. Somehow I remained untouched. I had no parents, no memory of them — so how could I cry? They never existed for me — so how could I feel? They were simply two bodies in two boxes.

Outside. The storm had increased. The rain lashed us. I was cold and miserable. The coffins lay forlorn in a hole in the ground. The man was speaking again. He stooped and threw mud on the coffins. It spattered. He looked at his hand. He wiped it on his handkerchief. We were leaving at last. Grandmother gripped my hand. I — .

I didn't hear her approach, but I sensed her closeness. I opened my eyes. She stood in the sunlight in front of me, watching. I squinted, smiled, patted the bench beside me and she sat. I took her hand and stroked it softly.

'Does this mean we are officially courting?' Susan asked lightly.

'I was dreaming. I wanted to make

sure you were real.' I found comfort in her presence, a warmth that was new to me. 'Have you often been courted? I bet you have.'

'Don't patronise me.' There was a rebuke in her words, but not her tone. 'I've told you. My course is set. At the moment I have no time for boys.' I felt her hand stiffen in mine. Her tone changed. 'I think you should leave Saddlebridge, Jimmy.'

I rolled my head to see her more clearly. A frown creased the skin between her eyes. I wanted to touch it. I asked her to explain and she shrugged.

'A feeling,' she said. 'I know why you are here. That is why I want you to leave. I'm frightened for you.'

I was touched by her concern and sincerity. I nodded towards the grave and her eyes followed mine.

'I've seen it before,' she said. 'Sad. I was just two weeks old when they died.'

'I was eight. And this is their resting place. I want to — but I can't for the life of me summon up much pity for my father. He wasn't a particularly good man. Oh, he didn't deserve to die like that — but still — I feel little kinship for him. My mother was different. She was a true innocent. I feel very close to her. And in a way I feel responsible for what happened.' I gripped her hand fiercely. 'It didn't occur to me until this morning. But she and I were in the house because I wanted to watch some senseless football game on the television. If — .'

'That is idiotic,' she cut in. 'You can't possibly blame — .'

'Oh, I must bear some of the guilt.' I wondered if my guilt was mere self-pity. I didn't think so. 'Anyway, I feel guilty. And no words can change that. I mean to have the bastard who butchered her!'

She wanted to know why I felt so certain the killer came from Saddlebridge. There was an appeal in her voice. I explained: old Charlie Grey, my own gut feeling.

'Robbie has a different opinion,' she countered. 'Nobody knows Saddlebridge like Robbie. They cry on his shoulder, pour out their problems to him. Yes,

200

Robbie would know if the killer lived here.'

I didn't point out that Robbie wasn't God. She wouldn't have believed me. And she wasn't making sense. She was warning me to leave, while at the same time saying the killer didn't live here, which meant I was perfectly safe. I pointed the contradiction out to her. Again, she shrugged lightly, flicked the hair from her eyes.

'I don't mean you are in danger from a double killer. No, Robbie explained to you. You are resented. The village wasn't a happy place to be just after the murders. And people have long memories. I don't think anyone would mean to hurt you, but they might. From spite — rage. And you are a reporter. They wonder what you will write about them.'

I felt a twinge of irritation. Warnings were becoming a familiar theme. I coldly asked if Robbie had sent her to find me.

Anger touched her eyes. 'No. He did not!'

I stroked her hand to convey my

apologies. I felt a fondness for this girl I couldn't comprehend; something that had little to do with sexual attraction; a strange emotion in itself for me. She glanced at me shyly, and the smile had returned.

'Let's go for a walk,' she said. 'Ten miles.'

So we walked. I was leaner and fitter. My limbs had ceased to ache.

* * *

'They take after my husband — your grandfather.' She sniffled, wiped the tears from her eyes. 'Everybody believed he died in the war, even Frank and Pete, but he didn't. He was no dead war hero. He simply didn't return. I don't know where he is now, or even if he is still alive.'

I leaned back, studied the cigarette between my fingers. The smoke drifted lazily to the ceiling. No air seemed to circulate around the old room, everything still and silent but for the sound of Uncle Frank in the garden. I was hearing the

202

truth. Grandmother had opened her heart at last.

'So I was alone with two sons to rear,' she was saying. 'I was proud of neither. Frank slow-witted, with an amiable clown's face that belied a streak of brutality and meanness; Pete quick of mind but possessing a massive capacity for slyness. But at least Pete was pretty. So it was easy to pretend. I fooled myself. How could a boy so beautiful be as bad as people made out? Frank was different. I couldn't fool myself there. Lumbering and clumsy. He grew from an ungainly child into an ungainly man. But I loved them both — and equally. Nobody can say otherwise.'

'Frank does,' I pointed out, trying not to sound callous.

'Oh, Frank is a whiner, incapable of rational thought in some areas. He was jealous of Pete. When they were young he beat him unmercifully. I couldn't allow that, but I couldn't bring myself to strike either of my sons. So I punished Frank in other ways. He often went without money, supper. Finally, he learned not

203

to use his fists on Pete.' Her head shook sadly. 'And Pete took his revenge for those beatings. He was sharp. He got Frank to do all sorts of stupid things, make a fool of himself.'

She pottered around the kitchen for a while, checked the oven, then took her seat again.

'So I made Pete into something he wasn't. I built a fantasy around him. My fine and handsome son. Then suddenly he was dead, and there was you.' No tears now. A touch of steel in her voice. 'My second chance. In a way Pete had been returned to me. But I wasn't about to make the same mistake twice. I wouldn't spoil you as I had him, no sweets every time you smiled. I'd make a man of you, nothing like your father and his brother. So I distanced myself from you. I didn't show you how I really felt.

'And I loved you. I didn't hate you. But you were eight years old, so how could I explain? I'd have to watch you grow, wait until you were a man and then you would understand. And you were not an easy boy, sulky and morose.'

Hell! There were good reasons to explain my behaviour; a child amongst strangers, who seemed to offer little affection apart from Frank. I didn't interrupt.

'And I never hated your mother. She was no better or worse than any other empty-headed girl her age. I never called her a whore. I never said you had bad blood in your veins. I never mentioned her, or your father. You didn't seem interested in them. And why do you think I bought the house in Livingstone Terrace?' I shook my head, numbed. 'It was the only way to make certain he married her. I forced him to face his responsibilities to her, and the child he planted in her belly. But I made sure the house wasn't in his name. I wasn't fooling myself there. If the house belonged to him I knew he'd play some trick or other. I charged them just a few shillings a week rent.

'And Pete always came back to me. I used to pretend he loved his dear old mum, and perhaps he did in his own way. I was the only one who listened to his problems and actually cared, who didn't simply go through the motions of sympathising. He needed me as much as I needed him. You may think me mad, especially after what I've just told you, but I still need him. And I'll keep that house and continue to visit until the day I die.'

And I understood more than she would credit me for. I had been to that house. I had experienced the impossible. She hadn't finished.

'When your aunt came she wanted to take you to Australia to join her family. I refused. Later, I had doubts. That night I sat by your bedside and watched you sleeping. I stroked your hair. I cried.

'Next day Frank went to pick you up from school. He returned in a panic. One of the other children had seen you leaving with a woman. Frank wanted to know if we should call the police. I shook my head. I realised who the woman was and what she was doing. I told Frank she was taking you a long way from here, that you were not returning. He was puzzled, but not perturbed.'

'If you loved me, grandmother — why didn't you try to get me back?'

She took her time answering. 'The night before I had reached the conclusion that your aunt was right. You should be with her and her young family.' She glanced to the window, infinitely sad. 'And Frank. Frank always hated his brother, and there was a meanness in Frank that was apparent to no one but myself. You had Pete's face. Sometimes I caught Frank staring at you in a way I didn't like. He followed you around like a puppy. Wherever you were, Frank was close, always whispering in your ear. I was frightened he might harm you. And myself? What if something happened to me? What if you were left alone with Frank? Yes, if your aunt had not taken you when she did, I would have contacted her, told her to come for you.'

The world was still mad, and getting madder. I smoked another cigarette. I asked about Frank's imprisonment. She showed no curiosity as to how I knew.

'It stunned me,' she said. 'Not that he got into trouble — but the reason. I might have understood if he'd lashed out at somebody who was tormenting him — but not that.'

I asked if my father had known that Frank had served time, and why. She nodded.

'He knew. He chided Frank about it. Frank would bunch his fists and storm from the house.'

I took a deep breath, and plunged. 'Did Frank murder my father, grandmother?'

She drew herself straight in her chair. There was no outburst as I'd expected. A simple and dignified response.

'I did wonder,' she said. 'Just for a short while. But no, Frank didn't kill Pete. The police questioned him often, especially the one who smelled oddly. But Frank was at the Fox that night. He never left. There were witnesses to prove it.'

There certainly were. But I didn't think much of Frank's alibi.

'And the day you returned,' she said. 'I

apologise for my behaviour. I recognised you. But I'd told myself you'd rush into my arms, tell me you understood. You didn't. I was angry.'

I stood, touched grandmother's hand, tried to impart a little comfort. She managed a weak smile. I glanced through the window. Uncle Frank worked on.

14

As was apt to happen whenever I set foot inside the Fox Inn, Sarah ambushed me in the passage.

'Guest upstairs,' she chirped brightly.

She disappeared back into the office before I had the chance to question her. I shrugged. I sensed no danger as I climbed the stairs and entered my room.

Dave Pearson lolled back on the bed. We greeted each other warmly. He commented that he hadn't set foot in the Fox for ten years, and Sarah had grown sexier with age. It was an opening for me. I asked how well Sarah had known my father. He whistled softly between his teeth.

'I expect even Pete kept his distance there, mate,' he said. 'She was young — and she belonged to George — even then.'

I shrugged. I still wondered about

Sarah and my father. I was sure something had existed between them. But what? It was a question that bugged me constantly. I asked Dave why he was here. He grinned, tapped the side of his head.

'The grey matter has been working overtime. I remembered a place we used to go to on our bikes as kids. Pete was a hoarder. He'd nick something and stash it away. Like to go on a treasure hunt?'

Did I! I had the door open, asked what we were waiting for. He sighed and bounced off the bed.

We used his van. We headed over the Peak towards the Sandford farm but didn't make it that far. We pulled off the road close to a small stone bridge. We got out, climbed the wall, and slid down the embankment. It wasn't much of a stream, more of a trickle, and the water was icy cold.

We were soon inside the tunnel, stooping to avoid the low roof. The walls were slippy and slick with slime. Our breaths vapourised before us. I blew into my cupped palms. Dave had begun to count, run his fingers along the edges of the stones, shake his head.

'One of these should be loose,' he said absently, and his voice echoed in the narrow space. 'But which one?'

He slipped a penknife from his pocket and opened the blade. He began to scratch against stone. The noise grated on my nerves.

'One of these buggers. Got to be.' He paused, pressed down and the blade met no resistance. 'This is it.'

It was taking an intolerable length of time. My patience snapped. I pushed Dave aside, worked with frozen fingers. I cursed when my thumbnail broke. I sweated lightly, but at last I had it free. I dropped the stone into the water and thrust my hand into the cavity, then my arm. My heart was falling. Then I felt it. It seemed to take an eternity to pull free; possibly no more than a child's money box with a coin slot at the top. It was locked.

We were soon back to the pale sunlight, then the van. Dave snapped the lock with his penknife, passed the box to me. He grinned. I had the honour of opening it. My heart thumped.

I found a yellow oil-skin bag inside, closed by a knotted string. I fumbled at the string with frantic fingers. The contents spilled in my lap. It was no treasure trove. A cheap diary, a single photograph, a brooch of seemingly little value.

I examined the photograph first.

Laughter exploded from my belly through my throat. I now knew how my father had blackmailed Hanson. I recognised the yard at the back of the Fox Inn. Hanson and a woman. He stood behind her, hands invisible inside her shirt, a glazed ecstasy on his face. And the woman? Well, without knowing her identity I'd have put her age at nineteen. But she was not nineteen, and not really a woman, possibly a mere thirteen when this photograph was taken — and her name was Sarah.

'Incredible,' Dave was saying. 'If Pete had shown this to George he'd have skinned Hanson alive, and worse, banished him for life from the Fox. And she was only a kid — jail bait.'

Exactly! I grinned smugly. I flicked through the diary. A lot of initials, a few sketches, some writing. I decided to leave it for a while. Something occurred to me. My father had worked the fiddle at the brewery, thieved with Dave, and God knows what else. So what did he do with his money. I asked Dave. He shrugged.

'I don't think he ever had much. We didn't make a bomb on the jobs we pulled together. How much he made with the brewery fiddle I couldn't guess. But when flush he really spent. Heavy with his fists, but generous with his wallet, that was Pete.'

The conversation lapsed; then I asked Dave if he could get hold of a shotgun for me. He sat bolt upright. He told me not to be stupid. I smiled.

'Oh, I don't mean to use it,' I said lightly. 'I don't want cartridges. An empty gun, that's all I need.'

We argued the toss. Reluctantly, he gave in, accepted the point I was making. But he wasn't happy.

Quite popular for once, later that day I found Robbie Sandford waiting for me. His face was grim as he followed me to my room. I took the bed and he paced about. He was coming to a decision. I waited. Finally, he found the words. They were short and to the point.

'I want you to stay away from Susan.'

The words stung and anger rose in my throat, but I wasn't really surprised. Doubts concerning Robbie Sandford had been festering in my mind for some time. I asked him to explain.

'You were seen.' He continued to pace, voice frigid. 'Holding hands, strolling about the village for all to see.' I asked what he was hinting at. 'I am hinting that you are not for Susan. That whatever is going on between you should cease. She is very young.'

'I'm not exactly an old man myself.' It was difficult to control my temper. 'And I've never so much as kissed her. Time you lifted your mind from the sewer.'

His fists tightened. His eyes bored

into my skull. 'I do not want Susan to associate with your sort.'

My sort! I wondered what the hell was my sort. I was no prize catch, but neither had I crawled from under a stone. And why the sudden switch? He was the friendly and affable man who had invited me to his farm to meet his family. If he hadn't, I would probably never have met his niece. So why this? Because I had the audacity to hold Susan's hand? And what was he seeing when he looked at me? Another man? A man who died seventeen years earlier? If so, why did that worry him?

I kept my thoughts to myself. I asked, 'Does Susan know you are here?'

'She does not. I know what is best for Susan.'

'You're a bag of wind,' I said heatedly. 'Susan is old enough to know her own mind. If she doesn't want to see me — fine. Or if her parents object to me — fine. But it has nothing to do with you.'

'We'll see.' He moved quickly to the door. 'We'll see.'

He had left, and I had one more puzzle to solve. Amiable Robbie had shown his nasty streak. Why?

★ ★ ★

I shivered and pulled my coat tighter. I pushed deeper into the shadows at the side of the cottage. The shotgun I had collected from Dave earlier hung limply in my hand. Midnight passed. Twelve-thirty. I thought of my bed — Sarah's body. I shook the images from my mind. Down and across the road the Fox Inn was clearly visible. No lights showed at the front, but I knew there was activity in the taproom. I cursed, waited, stamped my feet soundlessly.

At last!

A light illuminated the Fox Inn. The front door opened and closed and two shadows came my way. I heard the tread of their feet, heavy in the silent night. They halted not ten yards from where I stood. Sammy Kent shouted goodnight, Hanson reciprocated, came up the short path. Steel scraped on steel as he fumbled his key. The door creaked open.

I moved quickly.

I shoved him in the back, followed through and kicked the door shut. Seconds lost in finding the switch. The room flooded with light. I squinted, waited. He lay on his back and his mouth opened.

'What the hell — ?'

His voice froze as I pushed the shotgun close to his face, registered shock — then fear; a fear that possessed its own peculiar smell.

'Brings back memories, Vic!' I hissed. 'The dark. A door opening. A shotgun.'

'You're insane!' His gaze remained transfixed on the shotgun. 'For Christ's sake. What do you intend doing?'

'Blow you away, Vic,' I said coldly. 'Unless — .'

He inched away until his back came to rest against the bottom of the stairs. 'Say what you want.'

'What I've always wanted — the truth.'

I jabbed him with the barrel. A small cut opened on his cheekbone. He touched it, examined the blood on his fingers. It seemed to bewilder him.

I thanked God the gun wasn't loaded. If it had been — oh, hell! I'd have pulled the trigger!

'The fight, Vic,' I growled. 'Details of the fight in the Fox Inn. Everything!'

His head shook, not in reply, but to unscramble his brain. He wet parched lips.

'George,' he said quietly. 'Pete had the fight with George.'

I touched the end of his nose with the barrel, told him to start at the beginning.

'All right.' His voice was very low. I had to lean closer to pick out his words. 'Pete appeared around closing time. He was drunk when he arrived, and got drunker. I was there, George, Sammy, Frank, Robbie, and a man named Jack Bradley who died some years back.' The presence of Robbie Sandford that night interested me very much. Hanson talked on. 'Pete was stirring, but that wasn't unusual. Then Sarah came down the stairs. She said she couldn't sleep.

'She was dressed in tight pyjamas.' He

wet his lips again, but not because they were dry. 'Pete laughed and pulled her onto his knee. He talked dirty to her, touched. She looked to George to ask what she should do, though I'd say she was enjoying every moment. The room had gone quiet. We had an idea what would happen, saw the rage building inside George. 'What's this little baggage like in bed, George? Come on, enlighten us. Hot?' On and on Pete went, the beer doing the talking. Then George snapped. He dived over the table and went for Pete's throat. Bloody chaos. Sarah screamed, the old lady upstairs banged her stick, furniture crashed, but it wasn't much of a fight because they never got to grips. Somebody broke it up. Pete left soon after.'

'Why keep it quiet?' I asked.

'Don't talk wet!' Some of his confidence had trickled back. 'Pete died a few days later. It might have looked bad for George.'

'Sounds like a conspiracy to me, Vic?'

'Conspiracy to what? We didn't even have to discuss it. We knew what was right. We kept our mouths shut. Anyway, nobody asked us about a fight. It wasn't much to get excited over.'

I wondered. It was one hell of a coincidence that my father got himself murdered three days later. That I did know! And whether they had discussed their vow of silence or not, the men in that room had contrived to keep the events of that night hidden for sixteen years until Hanson let it slip out to a woman reporter. So why?

Hanson was struggling to his feet. I pushed him down. My action brought the fear back to his eyes. He pleaded that he had given me the truth. I didn't think so, not quite. I groped in my pocket with my left hand and held up the photograph.

'See the pretty picture, Vic. That's how my dad blackmailed you. She was a child at the time, Vic. And more than that, she belonged to George. You just told me how George reacted to the way my father treated Sarah. How would he have reacted if he'd seen this? And you one of his best mates. He'd have slaughtered you.'

Saliva bubbled from his lips. 'Pete put her up to it. Nothing happened. Only what you see. A quick feel when she pushed up against me. She dashed off just after, laughing. But George wouldn't have let me explain. He'd have gone berserk. When Pete showed me the photograph I had to do what he told me.'

'Did Sarah know about the photograph?'

'I don't think so.' He swallowed. 'Don't show it to George — for Sarah's sake.'

I wished he hadn't added that last bit. He didn't give a damn about Sarah. I looked down at him He was a blubbering wreck, seemed ancient, and some pity did touch my heart, but only a little.

'I'll ponder on it,' I said coldly. 'Is the photograph why you murdered my father, Vic?'

His eyes opened wide, head shaking. 'I didn't. I swear before God. And I don't know who did.'

It might have been the truth, it might not. I pointed the gun at his mouth.

His hands rose in supplication. I pulled the trigger and a loud click filled the room. I turned on my heels without glancing at him. I felt sick. I knew how the executioner had felt. Morally, I was the executioner. The gun hadn't been necessary, the photograph would have sufficed. I wondered if I was any better than the man who murdered my parents.

I was supposed to be tucked up in bed; the Fox Inn was bolted. I thumped on the door with my fist. Five minutes elapsed before the bolts clanked back. George's mood equalled mine. We argued, we swore. Each seemed to be waiting for the other to throw the first punch. Sarah appeared. George yelled to her to go back to bed. I was startled when she meekly obeyed.

We moved to the lounge bar, larger and eerie in its emptiness. George splashed whisky into two glasses, slapped them down on a table. We sat opposite each other, continued to glower.

I recounted my talk with Vic Hanson.

My voice was pitched too high, but I made no attempt to control it.

'Vic Hanson.' George chuckled drily. 'You must be a liar, squire. Vic wouldn't let you lick the froth off his beer if you were dying of thirst.'

'With a shotgun levelled between his eyes he might!'

George was thinking fast. His bushy eyebrows knitted in a frown. He had cooled. Now I had his attention, and interest. Our argument was over. He wanted to know exactly what Hanson had told me. I gave him Hanson's version of what happened in the taproom that Sunday night. He waited patiently for me to finish.

'And you think I'd have killed Pete because of the way he treated Sarah?'

'I think you might. That incident might have been the proverbial last straw. You saw something that night, understood something. Sarah's reaction. She enjoyed the way he fondled her. She didn't struggle. That's why you exploded.' I got no reaction from him. I went on, 'And I've done some

224

hard thinking. My dad spent some time with Sarah's mother. She told him what went on under this roof. Sarah was fourteen, don't forget, and you slept with her, sport. That's what my dad knew. But I don't think that was the reason you killed him. You were terrified that he'd take her from you. What — eighteen months and she'd be sixteen? He'd have taken her then, sport. His own marriage was a farce, he'd have ditched my mother sooner or later. So why not for Sarah? At least, that is what you feared. So no marriage for you. The girl you loved and had waited for all those years would be living with a man you loathed. You could have made it to Penningstone and back in twenty minutes, used the cellar as an excuse.'

It wasn't a real smile that creased his lips, more of a sinister leer.

'Guesswork and fantasy.' He leaned forward on his elbows. 'Now I'll give you something to ponder on, something Vic conveniently forgot. The night Pete came here. He was unpleasant at the best of times, but that night he really wallowed in the trough. The fight was merely the climax. Vic Hanson now — no love lost between him and Pete. Pete rattled him that night, poked him in the ribs and whispered. Vic turned white. Then there was Sammy Kent. At one time Pete wouldn't have dared go within range of his fists. That changed. I wonder why? And Robbie? He also argued with Pete. Oh, not verbally. But Pete passed the odd remark, innuendo — and Robbie's face darkened. And Frank? After the fracas with me — Pete thumped him in the stomach for no apparent reason and Frank took it without a murmur.'

Oh, hell. My mind was in turmoil. And was George giving me the truth? Yes, I believed him — every word. I believed he had given me a factual account of the events of that Sunday night.

George stood, loomed over me.

'Squire — you are squirting into the wind. Plenty with reason to hate — none that would have pulled the trigger.'

I watched him leave, heard his feet on the stairs. My face fell into my hands. The day had turned sour on me.

★ ★ ★

I sat at the table under the window. My eyes were gritty and sore. I worked through my father's diary again and again. The writing was cramped and often illegible. It went back almost thirty years. To some initials I could put names, to others I couldn't.

Dave Pearson earned several mentions. The jobs he pulled with my father were listed.

Vic Hanson was there, how he was coerced into helping with the fiddle at the brewery.

Uncle Frank was there, stating the reason he had spent those years behind bars.

No mention of George Slater; or Robbie Sandford, who by now I was very interested in.

The gem came with Sammy Kent. Good old Sammy rated very high with my father. I read it several times, almost drooled over it. Sammy Kent had a motive for murder, and it had nothing to do with the son who drowned.

With the arrival of dawn I laid aside the diary. I was exhausted, but ready to start another day.

15

The weather had turned again. The sky growled ominously, threatened the earth with a torrential downpour. I cornered Uncle Frank in his greenhouse. Another argument, more bitter words. I was tired, sick of the whole business. I wanted it to end.

'Something like that,' Frank was saying. 'But I don't know why he hit me. He was drunk.'

Wrong! Frank was a big man, a hard man. And he hated his brother. And they were men now, not children. He couldn't possibly be scared that his mother would send him to bed without supper.

'Why didn't you use your fists, Frank? Why allow him to humiliate you?' His head shook, words formed on his lips but didn't quite make his tongue. 'Because he knew you had served time and they didn't?'

His eyes bolted to mine. For a

moment I thought he might cry. He mumbled something about her having no right to tell me. I presumed he meant grandmother. I pressured him with more questions. His mind went off at a tangent, way back into the past.

'I don't know how it happened,' he said. 'I passed her on the street and she smiled. I thought she was one of those women, so I followed. It all went wrong when I approached her. She said things and I lost my temper.' He sighed. 'A long time ago now. I was so ashamed I wanted to die. I don't want anyone in Saddlebridge to find out. How can you respect a man who does that?'

Somehow, I couldn't summon up much interest, much pity. 'Did dad know?' I asked, though I already knew the answer.

'He knew. Tormented me with it. It was unfair. Nothing like that ever happened since.'

I'd heard all I wanted to hear from Uncle Frank.

* * *

'That's right,' grandmother said. 'Impossible to tell them apart at first sight. Identical: dress, figure, voice, face. But personalities — that was different. Ruth was bright and bubbly; Mary shy and studious.'

'Why do you think Mary left home — and so suddenly?'

'A real puzzle that.' Grandmother frowned. 'I told Robbie to ring the convents in the area — I couldn't think of any other place she might have gone.'

I didn't buy that theory. I prodded. 'A boyfriend?'

'Not Mary.' She paused. 'But — still waters run deep, or so they tell us.'

'And you could distinguish between them?'

'Not straight away. But, as I said, their personalities were different. I had no trouble when they came in here.'

Interesting. The bell over the door tinkled and a man entered. I thanked grandmother and left.

★ ★ ★

'I warned you to keep away!'

'I came to see you, Robbie,' I said coldly.

We faced each other at the back of the farmhouse. Robbie had just returned from the fields. He began to scrape the mud from his boots, his back turned so I couldn't see his face. I talked and he listened. I had finished before he faced me again.

'George is dreaming,' he said flatly. 'Pete and I got along fine. Any hint of blackmail is nonsense.'

I hadn't mentioned blackmail, but I let it pass. 'If I took a spade and began to dig in your hallowed garden — what would I find?'

His face showed no emotion, nor his voice. 'You would eventually arrive back in Australia — I imagine.'

'Smart answer,' I commented drily. 'I've worked something out. It concerns the twins. You made a switch, Robbie. I don't think Susan is the daughter of Ben and Ruth. I think her mother is the other twin — Mary. I think Mary died in childbirth. I think you buried her out here, created the garden around her.'

His smile disconcerted me. 'Dr Leigh. His surgery is in Penningstone. Why not visit him? He delivered Susan himself, in this very house. An uncomplicated birth. Ruth was fit enough to have danced the polka not an hour later. I think you should consult that doctor, seek his advice. You seem to be rambling. This fixation with your parents is warping your brain.'

If I had a brain. Foolishly, I pressed on. The smile on his face didn't falter.

'Even more bizarre,' he commented. 'And fair enough, I wouldn't have relished an unmarried sister of mine giving birth. I am not one of these modern people. I do believe it would bring shame on the family. And true — the permissive society was only in its infancy then. But the problem never arose. Mary was not pregnant. All right, she went away soon after Susan was born. I don't know where, or why. I wish I did. It will forever remain a source of anguish.' He paused, met my eye. 'Why have you come here with this preposterous tale?'

Why indeed? I gave him the truth.

'The night I was attacked — something made me duck as soon as I entered my room. My initial thought had been that there was a strange whiff in the air, a smell that didn't belong, then I decided it was the closed curtains that alerted me. I was right the first time. Pig shit. The whiff of pig shit in the air. It only struck me when I was talking to Sammy Kent about animal smells. And I asked questions. You were in the Fox that night. You left around ten; at least you left the taproom, but not the pub. You slipped upstairs and waited. You attacked me! I chased you but I didn't make a thorough search, merely threw open doors and glanced into the rooms. Easy for you to hide and leave by the front door while I argued in the taproom with George and the others.'

I still hadn't budged the smile from his face.

'There's more,' I said quickly. 'Take Sarah. People warned me off her, gave the impression that George was paranoid where she was concerned, but not you.

You told me she was fair game, that George wouldn't care if we didn't make it too obvious. You wanted me to make a play at Sarah. You'd have loved George to have a go at me, do your dirty business. And the inseparable four. Rubbish! You were no more than four boys of the same age.'

'You are sick, Jimmy,' was all Robbie had to say.

Perhaps I was, and I wasn't getting anywhere with Robbie. If I wanted to prove my festering theory it meant a return visit in the dead of night with a spade in my hand. I didn't fancy that one little bit.

★ ★ ★

I knew he'd be somewhere about!

Sammy Kent strode towards me as I left my car. I slammed the door shut, waited. He stopped stone dead not two yards away, suddenly indecisive.

'Run out of threats, Sammy?' I asked, showering him with a grin that twisted into a grimace. He hadn't.

235

'I'm here to put the record straight, sunshine,' he snapped. 'For the last time — nobody in this village had anything to do with Pete the creep's death. I'm sick of playing games. If you don't quit on this I'll break your back. You can push a man only so far before he snaps!'

I smiled, winked. Hell. It felt good to have this ugly ape's guts twisting in all directions. I tried to walk past but he spun me around. His face was dark with rage, and more, I read fear there.

'I'm going to tell you a story, Sammy,' I said calmly. 'It happened over twenty years ago. One day you had been away from your cottage and returned to discover the kitchen window broken. A real mystery; nothing touched, nothing taken. You shrugged it off. Then my father approached you. What he had to say scared the hell out of you.

'You had once boxed in the ring. Minor stuff, but sometimes you rated a small mention in the newspapers. You loved that. You saved the cuttings. But there was more. Other cuttings you kept were a little peculiar to say the least,

236

and you have an ego that can only be matched by your stupidity. You had come across some unsavoury characters while you were in the ring, and you have already demonstrated how easy it is to open a locked car, and perhaps that was your speciality. Anyway, the cuttings concerned a series of armed robberies. There were descriptions of the men wanted for questioning. One of these descriptions fitted you.

'My father didn't want money. He knew you didn't push a man with your temperament too far. His proposition was simple. You laid off him, and he'd keep quiet. It wasn't the villagers or grandmother who scared you away from him; it was what he knew of your past. And your son died through your own negligence.' I watched the muscles in his face tighten. 'You neglected him! So you needed a scapegoat to absolve your own guilt. In Pete Ellis you chose the wrong man. He wasn't the sort who would take a beating every time he crossed your path. He broke into your cottage to see if there was anything that might interest him. He found it in the press cuttings. You're a moronic ape, Sammy. Only a moron would have kept those cuttings.'

'Balls!' he spat.

'Bluster, Sammy,' I said coolly. 'Oh, you'll have burned the cuttings since, but my father kept a diary. I have that diary. Believe me, it will be child's play to track down the relevant newspapers.'

'Newspapers prove nothing. They — .' He clamped down on his tongue, then relaxed a little. 'Too long ago. Nobody will be interested.'

'I think they will. A policeman was seriously injured on that last robbery. They look after their own. The heat was on. That is probably when you decided to return to this backwater. As a motive to murder, seventeen years puts it much closer, hardly any time at all; memories were still sharp, witnesses younger. You murdered my father to silence him.'

'I took my time.' No pretence now. 'Pete Ellis died years after he broke into my cottage.'

'I've pondered on that. You gave me

238

the answer. A man can only be pushed so far before he snaps. He said something to you in the taproom the Sunday before he died. You realised that sooner or later he'd blurt out the truth. You decided to end it once and for all.'

I went for broke, 'Two more days to complete the article, Sammy. Then that and the diary will be on their way to my editor. You'll make the newspapers again, Sammy — the front pages. But this will be one story you won't feel like clipping out.'

I brushed past him and he didn't try to stop me.

* * *

I had worked steadily for three hours. There were five names on my list.

1. Frank Ellis. Motive — he had served a prison sentence for sexual assault — his brother knew.

2. George Slater. Motive — something concerning his wife Sarah — possibly he suspected she and Pete Ellis were lovers.

3. Robbie Sandford. Motive — blackmail. Something that concerned his sister Mary. What? I had no idea.

4. Vic Hanson. Motive — blackmail — the photograph of himself and Sarah.

5. Sammy Kent. Motive — Pete Ellis knew Kent had participated in a series of armed robberies.

And more. With the exception of Robbie Sandford, all openly admitted to hating Pete Ellis. And as Kent put forward — every man has his breaking point.

But hell! It read like a bad film script. Too many villains and nasties. And they all had the same alibi. All I needed to complete the script was a locked door and a missing key.

But still. One of these men had murdered my parents. I felt that in my bones, much the same as Charlie Grey had done before me. But which one? The one who came after me with a loaded shotgun? I shuddered. I knew that was the only way I'd solve this. And it was too late to chicken out now. With Sammy Kent I had already set the wheels in motion.

I'd already made a copy of my notes. I sealed them in an envelope and slipped them into my pocket. The original notes and the diary I pushed into the oil-skin bag which I hid in the bathroom.

Downstairs I found Sarah in the kitchen. We talked about nothing in particular, then I held up the photograph.

The blood drained from her face and distaste filled her eyes, and it shrivelled me. But still, in a cold voice I asked her about the photograph, if she had known it existed. She shook her head, and sat. Her voice was calm.

'I knew nothing,' she said. 'But let's go back to last night. George told me everything. The idea that he murdered Pete is insane. He had no motive. Okay, Pete provoked him into a fight that night, treated me as if I were a mindless doll. But George wouldn't kill for that. Pete and I were never lovers. I was a virgin on my wedding night — whether you care to believe that or not. But I can't deny that I was infatuated with Pete, that my heart leapt to my mouth at the sight of him, but he showed no interest in me.'

She glanced at the photograph. 'George was off someplace. Vic was in the taproom. Pete was here. Everybody knew how free Vic was with his hands. Pete whispered in my ear.' She paused a second. 'It was a game to me. I sidled up to Vic and asked if he'd help me with the sheets that were drying on the line. It was easy to manoeuvre him into the right position and get the expected result.'

Suddenly, her laughter filled the room. The old Sarah was back, and the distaste fled her eyes.

'And the glazed ecstasy wasn't on Vic's face for long. You can't see my hands in the photograph. They were doing what Pete told me to do. How I squeezed. Vic yelled and jumped into the air. I ran off.' She sighed. 'Stupid and childish, but that's what I was — a child in a woman's body. It earned me a reputation I never really deserved. As for Vic, he limped for a week, but his itchy hands were soon roaming again. And I didn't know Pete had a camera. I didn't know the photograph existed.'

I believed her. I even believed she went

to her marriage bed a virgin. And now she smiled at me.

'Nobody before you, sweetheart. The only man besides George. And you nearly got it right. It was because you looked so like Pete. I was fourteen again — filled with dreams — playing the role of temptress.' Her eyes touched the photograph. 'Do you intend showing that to George?'

'How would George react if I did?'

She shrugged. 'George has mellowed. I'd give him the truth and he'd believe me. He might even laugh. Still, I wouldn't like him to see it.'

I didn't answer. The photograph might be important. I slipped it into my pocket. And she had convinced me of many things, but not her husband's innocence.

★ ★ ★

'Okay. I'll check.'

Sergeant Cooper left the room, returned in the time it took me to smoke two cigarettes.

'Seems Charlie was interested,' he said.

'Mary Sandford. He put the word out for her, but she never turned up. And no, she wasn't reported missing by her family. Charlie was also interested in the Dr. Leigh you mentioned. Charlie spoke to him at the time. Ruth Smith gave birth at the farm, and Dr. Leigh was in attendance. No problems. And you were right about the other point you made.'

I thought I might be. It was hard to conceal my smug grin. I began to stand.

'Sit down, mate.'

There was a rough edge to his voice I hadn't heard before. I dropped back into my chair.

'Like to put me wise?' It was phrased like a question, but no request. He was demanding an explanation.

So I did a little explaining; not a lot, but hopefully enough to satisfy him. I told him I was simply delving into the background of some of the people I had met since I arrived in Saddlebridge, hoping for the flash of illumination that had so far eluded me.

He nodded grimly. He obviously wasn't

happy. He made it plain the interview was over. If I wouldn't come clean with him, why the hell should he care!

* * *

'And the pages that concerned me?' Dave Pearson asked.

'Shredded and flushed down the dunny,' I answered.

He nodded and relaxed, then his tone changed.

'You have to be out of your mind, mate. You believe one of these bleeders is a murderer. So what do you do?' His voice dripped sarcasm. 'Trot along for a cosy chat, just to tell them what you know. Where does that get you? Your neck in a noose — that is where! So I laughed, said it was a crackpot theory, but Pete and Jenny were murdered, somebody pulled the trigger. Maybe it was one of these five men. Let's assume you are right, and if you are — you just might be safe. After all, you can't prove anything. You need more than motive, and the killer knows that. But now you carry in your head the same information that brought about Pete's death. The killer might strike again for that very reason. You're in double danger.'

I had already worked this out for myself. In fact, I had set myself up as a target. I passed him the sealed envelope containing the copy of my notes.

'A precaution, Dave,' I said. 'If you haven't heard from me in a couple of days, do something with it.'

'Such as?' He couldn't keep the annoyance from his voice.

'Sergeant Cooper. Or, if he doesn't want to know, try the reporter I told you about — Larry Jenkins.'

'How'd you like some shells for that shotgun?'

I shivered. I tried a confident grin that didn't come off. 'No thanks. I'd probably blow my foot off.'

246

16

A heavy squall had turned the night black. The heat pumped into the car and made me drowsy. I squinted through the windscreen. The wipers droned monotonously. The headlights cut a wide swathe through the night.

I turned a bend in the road. A little further and the lights of Saddlebridge would lie below me.

I hit the brakes hard!

The car swerved a little as the brakes screamed and locked, pulled up no more than five yards short. I jumped out. The wind and rain smashed into my face, tore the air from my lungs. I ducked into it, reached and stooped over the figure.

This was all I needed! A bloody body in the middle of the road!

He lay on his side. In the glare of the headlights my shadow reached far into the distance. I pulled him onto his back.

I wondered if I had found a corpse.

My blood froze as the corpse grinned!

I felt the coldness of a gun barrel under my chin pushing me upright. He rose slowly, never taking the pressure from my skin.

'A little melodramatic, Jimmy, I admit, but effective.' He might have been chatting to an old friend about the weather. 'I saw it in a film and had to try it. It's been a long wait though, and you did drive that car a little too close for comfort.'

We had inched back to the car, faces close enough to kiss, separated only by the hardness of the shotgun. It forced my head back. I wondered if it would puncture the softness of the flesh under my chin, pierce tongue and brain. I now understood how Vic Hanson had felt the night I ambushed him — terrified!

He suddenly grabbed my collar and spun me around, slammed me against the cold wet steel of the car. I waited for death. I wondered if I would hear the explosion, experience pain.

I experienced pain!

My head split. Glistening tarmac roared up to meet my plunging face.

★ ★ ★

Drowning!

I gulped air. My arms floundered on the surface. My head shook violently. Then I lay frozen, ice on my skin. I shuddered the length of my spine.

'Come on, Jimmy.'

The voice stilled me. Consciousness began to stir. My eyes opened a mere slit. I lay in a cavernous room. The roof high above me. Light filtered through the broken slats, mixed with hazy drizzle.

And sweet Jesus! So cold!

I tried to move and the pain lanced through me. My head felt as if it had been pulped. Still, I let my eyes roam in their sockets. They took in the damp stone walls, the fireplace filled with rubble. I had the feeling of total emptiness, that I floated in a vacuum of pain.

'Come on, Jimmy.'

The voice was soft and I searched for the source in the darkness. I heard the

249

cackle of a short laugh. I had heard it before. One night, a distant and elusive image. A week? A year? Hard to remember. Hard to remember in a dream. I walked along a country lane at night. I felt good. Then the explosions split the night. And I ran, aware of the insane chuckle that chased me.

But sweet Jesus! This was no dream. This was reality.

I remembered! The body in the road. The pain that rocked my head.

Now he stepped from the deep shadows near the fireplace. I noted the smile on his face. He carried a shotgun in the crook of his arm.

'Nice to have you back, Jimmy.'

Ineffectually, I struggled to sit upright. My limbs seemed to be controlled by some distant force that had no connection with my brain. And so cold. I trembled. I glanced down. My legs seemed to belong to someone else. No feeling. I leaned forward to touch them. The insane cackling erupted again and I forced myself to look up at him.

Robbie Sandford retained the smile on

his face, but showed little emotion; no hate, no regret, no anger.

'Massage them,' he advised quietly. 'And behave, Jimmy. I don't want to tie you.'

That was considerate of him! I glanced around. The room was smaller than I first thought, probably no larger than the average sized living room. It stank of decay and neglect. I asked where I was.

'That needn't concern you,' he said. His eyes followed mine about the room. 'Some poor misguided soul once tried to make a living here. The land probably killed him.'

His indifference to me sent an uncontrollable anger roaring through my brain. I was an animal in a trap.

'Bastard!' I hissed through icy lips.

'That won't help you, Jimmy. But you have spirit — I'll grant you that.'

I wished I was able to stuff his patronising words down his throat. I wasn't. But at least my head had ceased to throb so violently, shifted into an area of dull pain. Some feeling had returned to my legs, tiny pinpricks of pain as I massaged them.

'Why am I still alive?' I asked.

'Things to see to, Jimmy. Can't have your body lying around for just anybody to find. We don't want another murder investigation, do we?'

It was weird. We might have been chatting across a table in a pub. And I realised I wasn't a human being to him. I might have been one of his animals awaiting slaughter. He might not take particular pleasure from killing me, but there would be no remorse — simply the nature of things.

I tried to stand. He laughed, told me not to bother. I slipped back to the wet floor as the shotgun rose to cover me. It fell as I did.

'I was right,' I said. 'I got it right.'

'Did you?' His smile covered me. 'Amuse me, Jimmy.'

I realised he was toying with me, but the need to talk was undeniable. The words fell quickly from my mouth.

'It still concerns Mary, the missing twin. Okay. She didn't die in childbirth.

But I came close. She was pregnant, and she came to you. Quite a problem. Your favourite sister with one up the spout! What disgrace to the house of Sandford! No shotgun marriage, if you'll excuse the expression. The man was already married. And no abortion for Mary. Unthinkable. So you hit upon your little plan. Ruth was already married to Ben, and as yet no offspring. Mary and Ruth were identical. You made a switch. Mary became Ruth, and Ruth became Mary, and making sure neither were seen around the village during this period. After the birth they were to have reversed roles. It went wrong. Mary took her own life. She was the mother who was to be denied her child.

'Of course, that was also a motive for leaving the farm. But I don't think she did. Mary wasn't the type. A quiet and sensitive young woman. She wouldn't just leave. And she didn't. And so worried about her — yet you didn't even report her disappearance to the police!

'And there had to be a reason for the garden. Such devotion. You turned it into a shrine. You only had to glimpse the expression on your face to understand that. Grandmother is the same. That gave me the clue. She clings to the dead; with her a son, with you a sister.

'And you made a mistake when you gave me the name of Dr. Leigh. I was supposed to think that good old Robbie has nothing to hide, and neglect Leigh. I didn't. And I can add two and two and make four. Why was Leigh only used that one time? The doctor who had attended your family for years suddenly wasn't good enough. For your sister's pregnancy you changed to Leigh. Why? I'll tell you. The family doctor knew Mary and Ruth intimately and would have spotted the difference. You couldn't have fooled him. Okay, Susan is born — now what? Another change of doctors. Leigh is out! It adds up. Mary was Susan's mother — not Ruth!'

I was exhausted after my little speech. I wondered how close I had come to the truth. Close, but his face said I wasn't quite there.

'The Sunday night at the Fox Inn,' I

went on. 'My father mentioned Mary. He teased. He knew the truth, or at least he knew that Mary was Susan's mother. He ought! He was the father. And it explains my feelings for Susan, why you warned me to stay away from her. Susan is my sister!'

'You arrogant animal!'

His expression had changed. I saw madness in his eyes, and I experienced a fresh terror. His boot smashed into my thigh. I choked down the urge to scream. The gun was pushed close to my neck. He loomed massively over me. The wrath of a violent God filled his voice.

'If Mary had carried Pete Ellis's child I'd have wrenched it from her womb with my bare hands. Susan is mine! I fathered her! I wanted her! I planted her!'

Oh, sweet Jesus. I couldn't believe my ears. I almost melted. His voice roared on.

'Mary and I were more than brother and sister! God blessed us with a special and divine love.'

Suddenly, he seemed to realise where

he was. He shook his head as if to clear his mind.

There were many questions I should have asked. But I was too numb, too shaken. Time drifted on.

'Can I get up, Robbie?' I asked. He shook his head, smiled. 'I need a piss — bad.'

He wasn't concerned. Then he shrugged. He nodded to the opposite corner from where I lay. He stepped back into the deeper shadows. I could no longer see his face, but the shotgun in the crook of his arm was clearly visible.

I took my time. I used the wall for support, half staggered to the corner, and went through the pantomime of urinating. I eyed the window only a few feet away; covered by sacking tacked to the sill. It flapped in the wind like a sail, offered a free passage from this hell house.

I turned back to Robbie, who hadn't moved; a motionless and headless torso.

If I was slow and he pulled the trigger he couldn't miss. But what the hell did I have to lose? My life was already forfeit.

'Go back over there, Jimmy,' he said. 'Don't put me to the trouble of tying you. That might annoy me.'

Annoy him! What did he think I was? A nothing? A docile cow waiting to be milked. I was more than that.

'One second,' I pleaded.

I stooped. I pummelled my thighs with the heels of my hands. I watched him from the corner of my eye. The gun hadn't risen to cover me.

I straightened. Two strides and I dived at the sacking. I tumbled into the night. Wind and rain lashed me. I crouched on my knees at the back of the building, shocked that I still lived and breathed. I glanced around.

I could make out the shape of the hills that rose above me, to my left a valley as it dipped away. I ran left. Downhill I plunged. I was disorientated. I almost blundered into a stone wall. I scrambled over it.

Eyes spinning, searching for lights, an inhabited cottage. Nothing. And there had to be a road or a track. He couldn't have carried me far. After he'd knocked me unconscious he must have driven me close to the building. My ankle caught and twisted. The pain howled from me before I could bite it off.

Still running. I slipped on the wet grass, rolled. Longer grass, bracken. I burrowed into it like a mole. The harshness of my breath seemed to fill the night. I stilled, listened. I looked up and scanned the ground in front of me.

My heart stopped.

Ten yards? Five? Hard to judge from this angle. He was a towering and sinister shadow that stalked me in the night. He knew I was close, but not my exact location.

'Jimmy,' he whispered.

Oh, my God! Had he heard me? I pressed my face into the wet earth.

'Jimmy? I know you're here. It's cold. Hear the wind? You'll die here. No shelter. The moors, Jimmy. Only ten miles from Saddlebridge but it might be a thousand. Another world. Let's talk this over. See if we can reach an agreement.'

Shit! Talk this over! With a shotgun!

That was his solution! And this wasn't the moors — I had enough sense to know that. I had an idea we were quite close to Saddlebridge.

And hell! He moved closer. He had to see me soon, or step on me. Was he blind?

Panic gripped me. I rolled. And I ran again. I waited for the pain between my shoulder blades. It didn't come. I stumbled, ran some more. I knew he was behind. Ten yards? Twenty? Another stone wall. I was over. My bloody ankle! I scrambled on my hands and knees along the side of the wall. I rested. My lungs refused to fill quickly enough.

Why hadn't he pulled the trigger? I kept asking myself. Twice he'd had the chance. Then I understood. He wanted me alive, at least for a while. He wanted me alive to fake my death. He had said as much back there in the building. So what had he planned for me?

I heard him climb the wall. A loose stone fell away.

'Jimmy,' he whispered. 'Don't make this hard on yourself.'

I wondered if I had imagined the hint of panic in his voice. And I could make him out, just, some twenty yards away. He faced directly ahead so he didn't know where I was, for now. And his reluctance to use the gun had filled me with new hope.

I was soon on my feet again, running. No pain in my ankle now. My arms pumped. I soared. I had wings on my feet. But he was still there, somewhere behind. My ears were attuned to the night. I heard his feet, his breath.

Then I spotted the headlights. They came and went as they followed some torturous lane into the hills. But I saw them! My speed increased. I hit the tarmac before I saw it.

A moment of panic. Which way? Christ help me — guide me.

Downhill once more.

Sweet Mary! I had guessed right. The headlights swept around the curve. I stood in the middle of the road and waved my arms. Brakes squealed. A Land Rover. I jumped aside before it hit me. I leaned on the side, gulped

260

air. I tried the door handle. Locked. I shook it. I screamed. The door on the other side opened and shut, footsteps.

'For the love of God,' I yelled. 'Help me, get me away from here.'

'Jimmy?'

I looked into his face.

Oh, he was a beautiful man my Uncle Frank. He had come for me. He loved me and I loved him. My arms circled his shoulders. I kissed his cheek. I hugged him. The tears flowed from my eyes. I had a million questions.

'How did you get here, Frank? How did you know? Robbie! He's a lunatic. He killed them. He means to kill me. Let's get away from here. He's up there someplace.'

Suddenly, I realised Uncle Frank hadn't moved, or spoken. I stepped back and studied his face.

I knew utter despair. I recognised something that had eluded me so long. I recognised truths and lies and deceptions. My mind went back.

I had left the hospital and moved to the post office. Frank was my friend then; at least, I thought he was; kind and attentive. He spoke of my parents, asked what I remembered of them. And I recalled grandmother of not so long ago, recounting how Frank was always whispering in my ear. That was true. He wanted to know how much I remembered. I gave him the truth. Why shouldn't I? I didn't remember my parents, or the events that led to their deaths.

I recalled how he patted my head, his exact words. 'That's right, Jimmy. They died in a car crash.' That's where I collected the idea from — Uncle Frank! Oh, hell. Even then he had been watching me, wondering if I knew who killed my parents, if my memory loss was feigned. After all, I might have peeped through the curtain, glimpsed the killer. And if I had? Well, I'd have met with an accident, young as I was, marked down for death even then.

And he was the one who spoke of bad blood in my veins. He was the one who poisoned me against grandmother. 'She hates you, Jimmy. She says your mother was a whore. Be careful of her.' Over and over he repeated it until I believed every word. He was the one who hated me, not grandmother!

And now I was back to reality. I stared into his face. I saw no pity, no remorse.

'Why are you doing this to me?' I pleaded.

'All my life Pete was there,' he said coldly. 'Then I was shut of him. But his wife died too. So there was you, his whelp, worming your way into mother's heart. I had been through so much and in you he returned to taunt me.'

I heard footsteps behind, the strain of heavy breathing.

'I under-estimated the little bastard,' Robbie grated, reaching us.

'You always were too cocky,' Frank spat back.

I was forced into the back of the vehicle. My head scraped on steel and I cried out, greeted by a blow to the side. The doors clanged like a coffin lid. I experienced the sweet kiss of oblivion and passed out.

17

Morning came and the storm had abated.
Afternoon, and shafts of pale sunlight
slanted through the broken roof. They
were taking no chances now. They had sat
me in my old corner, but my hands and
feet were tied. I was little more than a
useless lump of flesh. My limbs were dead.

With the morning Robbie and Frank
had gone. I had a new jailer, who I wasn't
surprised to see — Sammy Kent. He was
born for the role. When he grew bored
he'd come over to torment me. A small
kick here and there, nothing too drastic.
He didn't want me to pass out and spoil
his fun. At one point I asked what had
happened to the other members of the
gang — George Slater and Vic Hanson.

'You're a tosser, sunshine,' he said
cheerfully. 'You get no answers from
me. You go to your grave in ignorance.
But I'll tell you this — it took guts to
do what we did.'

Oh, hell. He was proud. This animal was proud. I no longer gave a damn if he booted my head in.

'Guts!' I hissed. 'You're a bloody baboon. You think it takes guts to blow a man to pieces — and a woman!'

He took a step forward, then stopped. He shrugged. 'She wasn't supposed to be there. But who the hell cares? She was nothing worth bothering about.'

I tugged on the ropes like a maniac. I felt them cut into my wrists. He howled his derision.

'That hurt, sunshine? My, I bet you were a real mummy's boy. I bet she petted you, kissed your rosy cheeks when she put you to bed.'

'Which one of you bloody heroes killed her!'

'Like I said — no answers from me, sunshine,' he said matter-of-factly. 'We planned it together. No significance who pulled the trigger. If it had gone wrong, if the executioner had been caught, the others would have gone down with him. We agreed.'

Executioner! Bloody madness! What

the hell was happening to me? The world was filled with lunatics!

Thankfully, Kent had decided to ignore me. I lapsed into a stupor. With evening Robbie and Frank were back. The three men went into a whispered conference. Robbie was the one to break off and come over to me.

'What did you do with Pete's diary, Jimmy?' he asked. 'And the article you've been working on.'

So that was the reason I was still alive. I should have guessed earlier. I had told Kent about the diary, and the article, knowing that if he wasn't the killer, word would soon circulate to the other men I suspected. I was a real smart-arse!

'Piss off!' I yelled.

Robbie sighed. 'You're making it hard on yourself, Jimmy. We've searched your room. We can't find them. Do tell us.'

'Are you my judges!' I screamed. 'Look at you. A punchy stick-up artist. A pervert. A lunatic who shunts one up his own sis — '

Robbie silenced me with his boot. I choked, coughed.

'The diary and the article,' he howled.

He wasn't fooling around. The boot again.

'In the post and on their way to my editor in Sydney,' I said quickly.

'Unlikely.' Robbie had calmed. 'You told Sammy the article wouldn't be completed for another two days.'

Oh, hell. I wanted to cry. I was even dumber than I imagined. I'd intended to smoke out a killer, not thinking beyond that, myself as bait. I was the bait all right. A bloody defenceless worm on the end of a hook!

'And we can wait,' Robbie went on. 'A day. A week. Look around — this room is all you will ever see. Feel the cold? You are shivering, and hungry, and thirsty. My guess is that by morning you will be happy to talk — so why prolong this? I believe they are hidden at the Fox. Not in the safe. You have deposited nothing there.'

'Piss off!'

Robbie sighed, turned to his friends. 'Show your faces at the Fox, and take another look around upstairs.'

I watched them leave. I fell into a fitful doze and it was night when I awoke, Robbie still on guard.

'What do you intend for me?' I croaked.

'Little pain, Jimmy. I do promise you that.'

It was the old affable Robbie I had first met; the genuine smile, the spark of friendship in his eyes. And I knew he was a lunatic. I listened to his pleasant voice.

'We've worked it out. You've been out of Saddlebridge for a while, nobody knows where. On your way back your car skidded — the Peak is a notorious black spot. You'll be drunk of course. An empty bottle in the car. There will have to be a fire now to obliterate the marks on your wrists. That is why I didn't tie you earlier.'

'My death has a familiar ring about it,' I commented feebly.

'Charlie Grey.' He smiled. 'Yes, we were responsible for that. But we didn't need to pour whisky down his throat. We simply ran his car off the road.

We followed him for days. We knew his habits. He whored and he drank. He didn't die instantly. But no problem. A simple twist of the neck.'

'He knew about your gang of worms — that you had conspired to murder my parents?'

'No.' He shook his head. 'Just me. He was interested in Mary. He had the same doubts as you — the change of doctors, why I didn't report her disappearance. He told me straight out that he believed I had murdered Pete and Jenny Ellis. Only problem was, he couldn't prove it. One day he stood at the back of the farmhouse and poked his toe into the earth, right above where she lay. I decided to finish it. I talked it over with Frank and Sammy and they agreed.'

He was insane! Three murders now. He didn't seemed concerned. He yawned, stretched. The hours passed slowly. I heard a vehicle on the track. The engine cut and a door slammed. Uncle Frank entered, triumph scrawled across his face. He handed something to Robbie.

'He hid it in the bathroom,' he said,

happy as a little puppy taking a stick to his master.

My heart had plummeted. A deathly chill rippled over my skin. I knew that for me this was the end. They would kill me now; coldly, efficiently. I heard their voices, the sound of tearing paper. A match flared. The splutter of flames taunted me. It was as if my life was evaporating with those charring shreds of paper.

In desperation I told them of the copy I had made — my talks with Sergeant Cooper and Dave Pearson in Penningstone. But my voice had risen to an almost hysterical pitch, words jumbled, and they didn't even begin to listen. They laughed and joked, and only when my voice trailed off did they become serious again.

'Sammy knows what to do?' Robbie asked Frank. 'He'll have the little bastard's car at the right spot?'

'Sure. I told him one o'clock — just to make sure. Nothing uses the Peak road at that time.' Frank checked his watch. 'Let's prepare him.'

Robbie suddenly fell on me. He wrenched my head back, forced my mouth open. Frank's face loomed over me. Liquid splashed my face, burned my throat, flowed into my stomach. I wanted to retch, couldn't. I thought I might choke, didn't. The nightmare seemed to go on forever before I passed out.

The cold air brought me round. I was aware of my feet scraping through the mud. I tried to scream but no sound came. I was pushed into the back of a vehicle; Frank's Land Rover, I think.

We bumped over the rough track, hit the smoothness of tarmac. We seemed to have travelled a long way, but probably hadn't, perhaps no more that five minutes before we stopped. I was dragged out. I tried to speak, to plead, but only managed to splutter incoherently. I was pushed into a car, positioned behind the wheel. It seemed familiar. My car! Somebody leaned over me. Somebody mentioned petrol, to make sure it burned.

'Step back from there, Sammy!'

I recognised the voice that barked eerily through the night, but my foggy brain failed to put a name to it. I felt the body lean deeper, grope, grunt. I understood what it meant. The handbrake! Mustn't let him release the handbrake!

'Back from there, Sammy! My last warning!'

The weight was off. I heard voices, feet. Explosions shook the air. Behind, the Land Rover burst into life. Its headlights brought sudden day as it skidded past. Then it was gone. Night again.

A shadow. A hand slapped my face, rocked my head.

'Wake up, squire. You're not dead yet.'

I squinted at the undertaker's rugged face, the cold eyes under the bushy brows. I had to be dreaming. There was a brown-haired angel perched on his shoulder.

18

Dave sat by the bed. He did everything that was expected of a hospital visitor. He ate the grapes and made the patient feel thoroughly miserable.

I was here for observation. Three long days. Something to do with the bumps on my head and possible internal damage caused by a reckless boot. I'd been interviewed by a Chief Superintendent from Divisional HQ, wherever or whatever that might be. I'd given him my story, and the next day repeated it to one of his subordinates. And now the police were through with me, hopefully.

My head still throbbed. I was a physical wreck, but apart from that I was fine. The sun slanting through the window helped.

Dave yapped on happily, and was already recounting his adventures again.

'The envelope you left was driving me mad,' he said. 'All through the next day I thought about it, then in the evening

I even discussed it with my wife. She told me to open it. So I did. It wasn't much, old cock. Nothing you hadn't told me already. But seeing it there in black and white was different. Sinister, almost menacing.

'I was in a dilemma. There was no way I was going to trot along to the bogie shop and make a fool of myself. So I rang the Fox. Sarah said you'd gone out the day before and hadn't returned. That shook me. When we'd talked you said you were heading back to Saddlebridge. So what the hell had happened to you? I tried to watch television but couldn't concentrate. Then I thought to hell with it. I was on my way to the Fox. It must have been after eleven.

'Only Hanson and George in the taproom. Well, I weighed into them. I demanded to know what had happened to you. There were some heated words exchanged before tempers cooled. I told them exactly what you told me, leaving out the bit about the photograph Pete took of Sarah and Hanson. They thought I was mad.

'Then Sarah spoke. Until then we didn't even know she had entered the room. And Sarah believed me, and you have her sharp ears to thank for your life.

'It seems Frank had been in around lunch-time asking if you'd left a parcel in the office for him. And there was more. Frank and Sammy Kent had left only minutes before I arrived. Sarah was clearing up in the lounge when she heard them leaving. They sounded excited and very pleased with themselves. Frank said something like, 'Have his car on the Peak road by one. Let's rid ourselves of the little bastard once and for all.' Sarah shrugged it off. She thought Frank might be drunk.

'George was all action then. He grabbed his shotgun. We walked, because headlights could be seen for miles. It was a hard half hour slog up the path in the dark, especially as Sarah insisted on coming along, Hanson acting like we were going on a picnic. But we reached the road.

'Hell! It was macabre.

'We got there just as Frank's Land Rover arrived. We watched these figures moving about. We couldn't see their faces clearly but we knew who they were. They seemed to be stuffing a dummy behind the wheel of your car. George soon cottoned on. He began to run. He shouted and Sammy Kent finally backed away from the car. Robbie decided to make a last stand. George was the better shot. Frank and Sammy made off in the Land Rover and we didn't try to stop them.'

More talk, then Dave left. I hadn't even thanked him, but he knew how I felt.

* * *

Two more days had passed. I sat in Penningstone policestation.

'You left us one hell of a mess to clean up, mate.'

'Sorry,' I commented drily.

'Sandford will survive,' Sergeant Cooper said. 'Kent and Ellis were picked up as they tried to board a ferry to

Ireland. Sandford is talking; sometimes coherently, sometimes raving like the fruit-cake he is.'

He offered a cigarette. I shook my head. I had smoked my last cigarette, a pledge I intended to keep.

'We've been putting the pieces together,' he said. 'Sandford and his sister had been lovers since their teens. I've spoken to the other sister, Ruth. She knew the situation of course. She says she didn't like it, but there was nothing she could do. Mary seemed perfectly content. Ruth herself married Ben Smith, a casual labourer in the district. They had been married several years without producing a child, though medically they were capable of doing so.

'Probably around this time Sandford decided he needed an heir. No discussion with Mary. She was his to do with as he pleased. His brain was already warped and God knows what was going through his mind.

'So, Mary finds she is pregnant. And whatever she thought of her incestuous relationship with her brother, by hell

277

she didn't want to bear his child. She decided to terminate the pregnancy without informing Sandford. But how? Her circle of friends was non-existent outside her immediate family. There was only one name she could come up with — Pete Ellis. Pete was a rogue, Pete knew everything, everybody said so. So she went to Pete and he gave her the name of an abortionist. And a real charmer was Pete. He'd have wheedled the truth from her, probably had her crying on his shoulder.

'Mary's mistake was going to the post office to withdraw her savings, yet she had to have money. Your grandmother mentioned it to Sandford. He confronted Mary.' Cooper spread his hands. 'She couldn't stand up to him — she told him she was pregnant. He was ecstatic, she horrified. He brushed aside her objections.

'You know what happened. The twins switched places. Ben and Ruth went meekly along with Sandford's scheme. As far as the world at large was concerned the child would be theirs.'

I swallowed the lump that rose in my throat. I thought of Susan, as I had done many times during these last few days. Gentle and sweet Susan. I couldn't help wondering how she had taken this, and I experienced certain pangs of guilt for being the instrument of such pain.

'So the child is born,' Cooper went on. 'Mary is in a bad way emotionally. Now she sees herself as a sinner. And she has to confess her sins. She isn't a Catholic, but she craves absolution; from the clergy — from the police. She wants to be punished for her sins. She fights with Sandford, who by now finds it hard to control her. In a fit of madness he kills her and buries her at the back of the farmhouse. The details are a bit blurred as yet.'

Oh, sweet Jesus, forgive us our sins. I felt like crawling into the deepest and blackest hole I could find, and staying there until death called me.

'Ben and Ruth Smith insist they know nothing of this,' Cooper said. 'They claim that to their knowledge Mary had simply packed her bags and left. Personally, I think they are liars.

'So we come to the night of the argument in the Fox Inn. Pete whispers in Sandford's ear. 'How's your nipper, Robbie? Naughty. Your own sister.' Of course Pete doesn't know that Mary is dead, only that she is the mother of the child Robbie is passing off as his niece, and that Robbie is the father. It hadn't taken Pete's agile mind long to work that out. And Sandford is stunned. Until that moment he doesn't know that Mary had been to see Pete. She kept that from him.

'Then there is the fight between Pete and George Slater, Pete's attack on his brother. Pete leaves and there is a babble of talk. I doubt if Sandford took part, but he listened intently, already plotting. He dismisses Slater as an ally; too strong-willed and independent, and Hanson's loose tongue makes him untrustworthy. Which leaves himself, Frank Ellis, and Kent. Next day he goes to work on them and they don't need much persuading. Through the years Pete had enjoyed the power his knowledge gave him. He thrust in the knife and twisted at every opportunity. Frank Ellis and Kent are two simmering powder kegs and Sandford is the fuse that is set to ignite them.

'They all want Pete dead, and say so, though none states his real motive. They all have something to hide from each other. A charming bunch of villains who acted out a fantasy, Sandford's fantasy, a plot from a bad film. They gave themselves code names:the executioner, the judge, the prosecutor. It was their way of absolving themselves from any moral guilt. The more we learn, the weirder it becomes.'

'Who pulled the trigger?' I asked.

'Kent. He was the executioner, Sandford the judge, Frank Ellis the prosecutor. In my opinion, more like Sandford the organ grinder, Frank Ellis his assistant, Kent the monkey who did the dirty business. Kent had some idea they were the three musketeers, all for one and one for all. It was an opinion not shared by the other two. If it had gone wrong, if Kent had been spotted and fingered as the killer, Ellis and Sandford would have denied all knowledge. And they'd have got away with it. And before he pulled the trigger Kent actually told your father he had come to carry out the sentence of the court. Pete thought it was a joke. He tried to laugh, told Kent to go to hell. Kent wasn't joking. He pulled the trigger. In some ways your father was the victim of a ritual killing.

'Now Kent isn't the brightest of individuals, but crafty, and devious. He didn't use his own car that night. He slipped out through the toilet window right onto the car-park. He had a car already marked, a banger that belonged to a young bloke who rarely left the pub before closing time. He slapped mud on the number plates and was on his way to Penningstone. A quicker and safer method than the one you used on your test run.

'Frank Ellis and Sandford were to supply the alibi. It turned out to be unnecessary. The bar was crowded; nobody knows who asked for the TV to be brought in, possibly no more than a piece of luck. You and your mother

282

were not supposed to be in the house, and that information came from Frank. None of the three were particularly distressed that Jenny Ellis had to die, unless it was Frank. It meant you would be moving to Saddlebridge.

'Old Charlie was on the scene. Sandford in particular interested him. Sandford spoke freely, didn't act as if he had anything to hide, which was in contrast to the other inhabitants of Saddlebridge. So Charlie plugged away at Sandford without making it too obvious to anyone but Sandford himself. There was as yet no garden at the back of the farmhouse to illuminate his way, but Charlie smelled a rat concerning Sandford and the missing sister. Sandford called his little gang of sewer rats together for a pow-wow, maybe another trial, and they dealt with Charlie, as easy as that. They knocked off a senior police officer and not for a second did anyone suspect anything. Again it was Kent who did the actual business.

'Seventeen years later an Australian ragbag appears out of the blue.

'Sandford and his gang wanted you out of the village, and they had countless accomplices. You were an interloper picking away at ancient scabs, and more, a journalist. George Slater's antipathy is easily answered away; he saw you as an arrogant jackass, the likeness of your father, and that meant trouble.

'Sandford offered the greasy hand of friendship. He wanted you to confide in him so he could maintain a close check on whatever progress you made. It turned sour almost immediately when Susan brought out the family album. His reaction was swift. He fired those shots over your head to scare you from the village.

'Kent joined the fun. He slopped whitewash over your car, and dumped the dead cat in your room. And you had begun to pester Frank. He came to your room to allay some of your suspicions, give you as much of the truth as he dared. He needed the whisky because your mere presence was a physical torture to him.

'Sandford attacked you. A frightener. He didn't intend to damage you too badly at this stage. With Sarah down the landing and George below he didn't mean to get involved in a fight. He meant to knock you unconscious with a single blow.' Cooper smiled. 'That whiff of pig shit saved you from waking up with a nasty headache.

'Once you were close, mentioned that Pete kept a diary that was now in your possession, they decided to finish you; and you had been seen holding Susan's hand, which tore Sandford's insides to shreds. And just perhaps if Sandford had known his own name wasn't in the diary, that Pete hadn't brought it up to date, it might have been different, but I doubt it. The blood lust was on him.

'They set up the ambush. They knew you'd driven to Penningstone and decided to grab you on your way back. You passed Frank in the darkness. He signalled to Sandford, who did his body in the road act. They needed you alive, at least until they had the diary and the article you were supposed to be writing.

'Sandford and Ellis drove you to the abandoned farmhouse in Ellis's Land

Rover. They couldn't get your car up there. Kent stashed it in his garage. By using the back lanes he was able to avoid prying eyes, and those of his nosy neighbour. They had already arranged what to do when they found the diary and article. Ellis took them to Sandford, and they rendezvous'd on the Peak road with Kent. They reckoned without Sarah Slater and her sharp ears.'

I leaned back and wondered if it had all been worthwhile: the pain, the heartache. I shook hands with Sergeant Cooper, thanked him for his help and patience.

★ ★ ★

My bags were packed and lay on the bed. Sarah stood by the door. She asked what I intended doing now.

I shrugged. I was on my way back to Australia, police permitting. I intended to write my story, flog it to the highest bidder, then go walkabout in Queensland for a while. I didn't want to think beyond that. I had offered to stay with grandmother but she had firmly shaken her head, and I have to admit, much to my relief. The brooch I had found with my father's diary belonged to her. She had always believed that Frank had stolen it. She cried when I gave it to her. She had vowed to stick by her son, visit him in prison. There was no hate in her heart for Frank, only an aching emptiness. She had decided to sell the house in Livingstone Terrace.

And now, I had no words for Sarah. I kissed her cheek and held her close for a few moments, and that seemed to convey all my thoughts and emotions for her. I slipped the photograph of herself and Hanson into her palm.

I carried my bags downstairs, pushed open the office door. George still scowled, still detested the sight of me.

'I'm leaving, sport,' I said, getting no reaction. 'I'd like to thank you.'

'That's okay, squire.'

He was bloody impossible! I simply wanted to thank the man for saving my life, and to him it was of no more importance than relieving an itch. My temper bubbled to the surface. All the old animosity returned.

'How long have you known about those three?' I asked.

'I didn't, squire!' He glared with that undertaker's face, then a sudden weariness filled his voice. 'I had my suspicions at the time, especially when that copper began to stick his nose in. But in those days suspicions were the natural way of life. We all suspected somebody. I thought it just might be one of the men in the taproom the Sunday night before Pete died. Some harsh words were spoken after he left, and that's a fact, why we kept the events of that night secret. It was possible one of them might have killed Pete in a fit of rage if he'd been pushed too far — I'd come close to that myself — but not Pete's wife — not a woman! Christ, no!'

I left him without another word.

I was outside, looking towards the village; empty as if the plague had struck. I turned to look at the inn one last time. This was where it began, the night my drunken father whispered those few unguarded words into the ear of Robbie Sandford, that prophetic invitation to die.

I had regrets. Vic Hanson. I regretted what I had done to him at his cottage that night. He was nothing more than a harmless little lecher who liked to parade in uniform. He had been the victim of my father's greed. At one point I had almost dismissed him as a suspect. If he had been the killer, he'd have made sure he had the photograph before he pulled the trigger, and once he had the photograph, would there be any point in pulling the trigger? But then, he might have gone to the house with the intention of forcing my father to give him the photograph at gunpoint. And if my father had made a grab for the gun? Well it was feasible, and at least explained away why the killer argued on the doorstep with my father, always a mystery in itself. How the hell was I to know it was Sammy the head-case passing sentence?

And Saddlebridge?

I guessed Saddlebridge was just unlucky. At one point in its history it had thrown together Robbie Sandford, Sammy Kent and Frank Ellis. Three murderous bits of scum: a lunatic, a head-case, and a man warped by jealousy for a brother. My father had been the catalyst that drew them together, and set them on a trail of murder. And Saddlebridge had its good side: George and Sarah Slater, grandmother, even its former inmate Dave Pearson — the crooked lad who went straight.

The gravel crunched under my feet and I tossed my bags into the back of the car. Near the summit of the Peak I thought I glimpsed a figure. I wondered if it might be Susan. I'd return one day — to see her — to check if she'd become that doctor. And if she hadn't, if she'd remained single and wasn't the mother of five sets of twins — well — I might just —

I was over the bridge that was the gateway to Saddlebridge. I had survived, laid the ghost of my past and the deaths of my parents; the crucifix around my neck was my talisman to the future, my guardian against the nightmare that stole through my mind in the dark. And I knew one thing above all others — a dedicated cop would have been proud of me.

Rest easy in your grave, Charlie; your haunting days are done.

THE END

A LANCE FOR THE DEVIL
Robert Charles

The funeral service of Pope Paul VI was to be held in the great plaza before St. Peter's Cathedral in Rome, and was to be the scene of the most monstrous mass assassination of political leaders the world had ever known. Only Counter-Terror could prevent it.

IN THAT RICH EARTH
Alan Sewart

How long does it take for a human body to decay until only the bones remain? When Detective Sergeant Harry Chamberlane received news of a body, he raised exactly that question. But whose was the body? Who was to blame for the death and in what circumstances?

MURDER AS USUAL
Hugh Pentecost

A psychotic girl shot and killed Mac Crenshaw, who had come to the New England town with the advance party for Senator Farraday. Private detective David Cotter agreed that the girl was probably just a pawn in a complex game — but who had sent her on the assignment?

THE MARGIN
Ian Stuart

It is rumoured that Walkers Brewery has been selling arms to the South African army, and Graham Lorimer is asked to investigate. He meets the beautiful Shelley van Rynveld, who is dedicated to ending apartheid. When a Walkers employee is killed in a hit-and-run accident, his wife tells Graham that he's been seeing Shelly van Rynveld . . .

TOO LATE FOR THE FUNERAL
Roger Ormerod

Carol Turner, seventeen, and a mystery, is very close to a murder, and she has in her possession a weapon that could prove a number of things. But it is Elsa Mallin who suffers most before the truth of Carol Turner releases her.

NIGHT OF THE FAIR
Jay Baker

The gun was the last of the things for which Harry Judd had fought and now it was in the hands of his worst enemy, aimed at the boy he had tried to help. This was the night in which the past had to be faced again and finally understood.

PAY-OFF IN SWITZERLAND
Bill Knox

'Hot' British currency was being smuggled to Switzerland to be laundered, hidden in a safari-style convoy heading across Europe. Jonathan Gaunt, external auditor for the Queen's and Lord Treasurer's Remembrancer, went along with the safari, posing as a tourist, to get any lead he could. But sudden death trailed the convoy every kilometer to Lake Geneva.

SALVAGE JOB
Bill Knox

A storm has left the oil tanker S. S. *Craig Michael* stranded and almost blocking the only channel to the bay at Cabo Esco. Sent to investigate, marine insurance inspector Laird discovers that the Portuguese bay is hiding a powder keg of international proportions.

BOMB SCARE — FLIGHT 147
Peter Chambers

Smog delayed Flight 147, and so prevented a bomb exploding in mid-air. Walter Keane found that during the crisis he had been robbed of his jewel bag, and Mark Preston was hired to locate it without involving the police. When a murder was committed, Preston knew the stake had grown.

STAMBOUL INTRIGUE
Robert Charles

Greece and Turkey were on the brink of war, and the conflict could spell the beginning of the end for the Western defence pact of N.A.T.O. When the rumour of a plot to speed this possibility reached Counter-espionage in Whitehall, Simon Larren and Adrian Cleyton were despatched to Turkey . . .

CRACK IN THE SIDEWALK
Basil Copper

After brilliant scientist Professor Hopcroft is knocked down and killed by a car, L.A. private investigator Mike Faraday discovers that his death was murder and that differing groups are engaged in a power struggle for The Zetland Method. As Mike tries to discover what The Zetland Method is, corpses and hair-breadth escapes come thick and fast . . .

DEATH OF A MARINE
Charles Leader

When Mike M'Call found the mutilated corpse of a marine in an alleyway in Singapore, a thousand-strong marine battalion was hell-bent on revenge for their murdered comrade — and the next target for the tong gang of paid killers appeared to be M'Call himself . . .

ANYONE CAN MURDER
Freda Bream
Hubert Carson, the editorial Manager of the Herald Newspaper in Auckland, is found dead in his office. Carson's fellow employees knew that the unpopular chief reporter, Clive Yarwood, wanted Carson's job — but did he want it badly enough to kill for it?

CART BEFORE THE HEARSE
Roger Ormerod
Sometimes a case comes up backwards. When Ernest Connelly said 'I have killed . . . ', he did not name the victim. So Dave Mallin and George Coe find themselves attempting to discover a body to fit the crime.

SALESMAN OF DEATH
Charles Leader
For Mike M'Call, selling guns in Detroit proves a dangerous business — from the moment of his arrival in the middle of a racial riot, to the final clash of arms between two rival groups of militant extremists.